PRAISE FOR CHRIS LYNCH

Kill Switch

★"A compact, frayed-nerves bundle of brilliance."
—*Booklist*, starred review

"A great premise, developed with brilliant prose. . . .
Characters are sympathetically and vividly evoked, and the brief
novel is a model of good writing."—*Horn Book*

"A psychological exploration that leaves readers with just as many
interesting questions as answers."—*SLJ*

Angry Young Man

★"For those who wonder about the roots of homegrown terror and
extremism, National Book Award Finalist Lynch pushes the spotlight
from the individual to society in a story that can be brutal and ugly,
yet isn't devoid of hope."—*Publishers Weekly*, starred review

★"Well paced and provides an eerie look into the small town of
repressed aggression in which the boys grew up. . . . A quick read, but
one that will stay with readers long after it's over."
—*SLJ*, starred review

Inexcusable

National Book Award Finalist

★"Lynch has hit a home run with this provocative,
important read."—*Kirkus Reviews*, starred review

★"Through expertly drawn, subtle, every-guy details, Lynch creates
a nuanced, wholly believable character that will leave many readers
shaking with recognition. . . . Unforgettable."—*Booklist*, starred review

"This raw and powerful book will hammer its way into
your heart and haunt you. The world needs this story.
And you want to read it—trust me."
—Laurie Halse Anderson, author of *Speak*, a Printz Honor Book

ALSO BY CHRIS LYNCH

Inexcusable
Angry Young Man
Kill Switch
Iceman
Pieces
Shadow Boxer
Freewill
Little Blue Lies

CHRIS LYNCH

GYPSY DAVEY

SIMON & SCHUSTER BFYR

New York   London   Toronto   Sydney   New Delhi

SIMON & SCHUSTER BFYR

An imprint of Simon & Schuster Children's Publishing Division

1230 Avenue of the Americas, New York, New York 10020

Text copyright © 1994 by Chris Lynch

Previously published in 1994 by HarperCollins

Cover photograph copyright © 2014 by Saul Landell/mex/Getty Images

For information about special discounts for bulk purchases, please contact Simon & Schuster Special Sales at 1-866-506-1949 or business@simonandschuster.com.

The Simon & Schuster Speakers Bureau can bring authors to your live event. For more information or to book an event, contact the Simon & Schuster Speakers Bureau at 1-866-248-3049 or visit our website at www.simonspeakers.com.

Also available in a SIMON & SCHUSTER BFYR hardcover edition

Cover design by Krista Vossen

Interior design by Hilary Zarycky

The text for this book is set in Berling.

Manufactured in the United States of America

First SIMON & SCHUSTER BFYR paperback edition March 2014

2 4 6 8 10 9 7 5 3 1

The Library of Congress has cataloged the hardcover edition as follows:

Lynch, Chris, 1962–

Gypsy Davey / Chris Lynch. — First edition.

pages cm

Previously published in 1994 by HarperCollins.

Summary: Twelve-year-old Davey is the man of the household, taking care of his mother and older sister as best he can and avoiding them when they are either too mean or too sad.

ISBN 978-1-4424-7284-6 (hardcover) — ISBN 978-1-4424-7287-7 (eBook) — ISBN 978-1-4424-7285-3 (pbk.)

[1. Family problems—Fiction. 2. Single-parent families—Fiction. 3. Brothers and sisters—Fiction. 4. Mothers and sons—Fiction.] I. Title.

PZ7.L979739Gy 2014

[Fic]—dc23

2012049522

CONTENTS

Two Too Many / 1

Motion / 4

Sumpin' Nice / 12

Like a Bird Out of Water / 23

Love, Sister, It's Just a Kiss Away / 27

Decked Out in Cheese / 40

Muthuh / 56

They / 64

Gimp / 68

Regular Cool / 76

Big Now / 82

Us Alone Happy / 93

Come Dancing / 95

For the Good Times / 114

Lessa Lester / 121

Goin' Where the Water Tastes Like Wine / 125

Great Things in Convertibles / 132

Hysterical / 144

Until He Couldn't See It Anymore / 148

Like Hell to Pieces / 150

TWO TOO MANY

My sister Joanne has a baby and sometimes after school I go over there and I help her with it and she lets me have a glass of wine and then I start to think of things.

Things like that I'm really good with babies even though I'm only twelve and I can think of no reason why I should be after all good with babies since I don't have any of my own but I sure would like to. Better than my sister is with her own baby that's for sure though I don't actually mean to be mean because she's nice to me some of the time and it's hard for her and I fully understand that. She's only seventeen herself but her old man she calls him is thirty which is why there's always a glass of wine around although from what I can see the old man himself ain't. Around that is.

Sometimes my sister goes out right away when I come

over and comes back hours later when me and the baby Dennis are asleep. She says that Dennis is crazy because he's loud and he's active and he doesn't listen but then he stops still and stares for almost ever and he makes a lot of sounds that are nothing at all like words and he moves funny sometimes more like a praying mantis than like a big baby boy and that all this is why little Dennis and me get along so good is what she says because we're both screwed she says. And that's why she has to leave sometimes.

But I don't see the problem so much to be honest and I tell my sister so. She says I can't see it because I'm a retard myself is what she says when she's not feeling so nice or just that Davey you don't understand things very well is what she says when she's better.

But I can do things. I can change Dennis's diaper when he needs it, and I know when he needs it. I even like it doing the changing doing the feeding like it when my sister leaves us alone because I like being the one in charge for a change. I am really responsible and I don't think my sister changes Dennis often enough because of what I see sometimes on his little bum. Like boils. I can't tell my sister something like that because I told her once told her after she came home from a long long time when she was out of the house. And she said how dare you to me and she hit me slapped me real hard. Then she stared at me and thought about it and just said how dare you again and hit me real hard on the same part of my face again even though I'm bigger than she is by a lot. But I couldn't do nothing about it of course because I couldn't. Except cry. I could cry and I did just with the water part and no sound coming out of me. And I turned so little Dennis couldn't see because he looks up to me admires me and he's real curious and kept stretching his neck to try to see me. So now I just wipe the cream on him all the time and I blow lightly on the red parts of his bottom to cool him because it looks hot.

My sister says so what to all this because she did it all for me when I was little like our brother Gary who doesn't live around here anymore did for her because she says Mom had two kids too many than she could handle. And so I owe somebody.

MOTION

Joanne was seven years old when she became, in effect, mother by default for Davey, who was two. That was the year Lois, their mother, started packing Joanne off to school in the morning with her lunch of a hot dog wrapped in a piece of bread, a bag of Cheetos, and a two-pack of Suzy Q's. Following breakfast of one Pop-Tart, which the girl could either eat or not, Joanne would take a last look over her shoulder as Lois plunked Davey down in front of the TV.

Which was where Joanne would find her brother when she came back in in the afternoon.

"Take the long route home?" Lois said as she snatched her wet-look leather jacket off the coat tree. "Make sure Davey has something to eat at some point. He won't eat for me today." And she was gone.

"You didn't eat *nothing?*" Joanne said as Davey finally looked away from the screen and noticed her. He let out a squeal and held his hands straight up in the air as she ran over and lifted him up. They played their game, where she let go of him and he hung on by holding tight around her neck, as they headed right for the kitchen. Davey laughed "like a madman," Joanne said, even though it took all his strength to hold on, and even though he fell to the floor hard more than once.

The ritual. It became the one reliable good time of the day, when Joanne made orange macaroni and cheese out of the box. He ate his share, at least half a box, every time, no matter how his mother said he'd eaten all day. Joanne ate with him, out of boredom, out of comradeship, out of whatever need still gnawed at her belly every afternoon after she finished her lunch. It started to show on both of them, the daily macs, as Joanne got more and more chunky while Davey grew like a sunflower, tall and taller and ragged and unsteady.

"Can't you do something else, Davey? Don't you want to?" she first asked him when she was ten and his TV watching schedule was interrupted each day only by two and a half hours of kindergarten.

"Ya," he answered enthusiastically, but shrugged while doing it. It was becoming common, the mixed communication, like when he'd say "yes" to something while shaking his head, or "I don't know" while nodding.

"Well then come with me," Joanne said as he jumped on her back, the new daily ritual since he'd become too big for her to carry. They ate their macaroni, then she dressed him in his winter jacket, ski mask, and mittens.

Finally, she took him by the hand to the places she always went. To get away from the place she would teach him to get away from. She took him to the library, where she read him picture books until he got bored and started wandering, pulling books down. Where Joanne's friend Isobel, the librarian, came over and corralled Davey back into the chair, loosened his heavy clothes in the stuffy library air, immediately relaxing him. Isobel read to them from *The Wind in the Willows*, and both children sat still until things got too busy and she had to get back to work.

She took him to the cobbler's shop, where *nobody* ever seemed to go anymore even though Vadala the shoe guy was completely surrounded, up one wall and down the other, with old black shoes. Joanne and Davey had a ball clomping up and down the old dry floorboards wearing fifty different people's shoes. "They need a walk. Take 'em for a walk," Vadala would say. He loved it and tugged away at a full white mustache growing down over his lips, pushing biscotti and hard candies on the two kids as they paraded by his bench.

Joanne could go on the whole day walking the shoes, and many days she did. But for Davey the big thrill came with the workbench. Vadala set him up with tacks, a hammer, and a rubber sole, and that was the last they saw of Davey's face. Hammering away like old John Henry, Davey was motivated. He pounded, harder and harder, faster and faster, louder and louder, letting out the occasional grunt of effort, the occasional giggle of delight. He worked so long at that hammering that even Joanne stopped her marching to join Vadala in just staring at Davey. When she finally had to pull him away to leave, there were droplets of sweat rolling off the tip of his nose.

Davey was so supercharged by that time, he couldn't even stay in his seat during most of the bus ride Joanne took him on. It was the long straight ride up Washington Street, her favorite of the many regular routes she rode just for the riding. For the *motion* that had become so important to her, the perpetual, numbing hum of motion. She would let her temple loll against the window as she looked over at whatever passed by. The vibration in her head such a nice soundtrack.

She would let him roam since, as usual in the afternoon, there were only a couple of old people on the bus who didn't want any trouble. But Joanne would break her own peace whenever Davey was too close, and too hard, on the driver's ear.

"Sit down, Davey, I want you to look at this," she said, jamming him into her prized window seat. "There." She pointed to a brown triple-decker with the porches about to drop to the sidewalk. "There is where we lived when you were born." Davey stared silently at that house and at all the other rotting triplets that floated by. "And there," she said one minute later, "is where we lived when I was born. And that one there is where we moved to right after, and that empty lot there used to be the house we lived in just two years ago."

Davey listened but didn't react much except to say "uh-huh," and "oh." He was nevertheless spellbound. By the same thing that brought Joanne back to the buses to nowhere day after day. The houses flying by, the neighborhoods melting away, popping up, one blending into another, the wheezy growl of the bus engine that sounded like it was just sitting right there in the rear seat of the bus instead of outside, and didn't sound like any other sound. Davey leaned his temple against the glass, and she knew she'd done something for him. Joanne got up out of the inside seat, swung around to the window seat right behind her brother's, and assumed the identical position. They didn't move when the bus pulled into the station, waited fifteen minutes, then headed back up Washington Street to where they came from.

Joanne had to shake Davey, then pull him, when it was time to get off the bus. Then all the way up the street toward home he was excited, agitated, like an animal needing to run. Joanne hadn't seen much of this in Davey before, but she liked it, saw it somehow as a good thing even if she wasn't sure why. She wanted to take him out some more, to let him run, to simply stand and watch him do it, but it was starting to get dark and they had to get home. One time she grabbed him in a bear hug, his arms flattened to his sides, to play at restraining him. He kicked and twisted until finally he exploded out of her arms and sprinted, Joanne laughing and pursuing him.

"Get your little ass in here," Lois growled as she threw the front door open.

"What, Ma? What?" Joanne pleaded, already trembling as she followed her mother's backward steps. When they'd all gotten inside, Davey, bringing up the rear, turned and shut the door.

"Where the *hell* have you been?" Lois screamed, smashing Joanne on the side of the head with the heel of her hand. "Who the *hell* do you think you are, Joanne? The boss? Are you the boss around here now? I was worried *sick*." Every time she said "hell," or "sick," or "boss," or "child," she slapped Joanne in the same spot, the patch of the cheek that was already pink from the outside air. "You think you can just take this child, and whisk him away when you feel like it, like a toy?"

Joanne stood frozen, still in her knee-length navy-blue coat. Her nose ran almost as fast as her tears, over her lips, her chin. "I thought he might like to go out," she whimpered. Davey stood behind her, clutching the coarse wool of her coat like a bat.

Lois leaned right down into Joanne's face. "You mean you thought *you* might like to go out." Joanne turned her face half away, not all the way away because she was afraid of offending her mother. But she had to turn, not so much from the words as from the odor, of men's cologne, of something bitter, of onions and sweat and smoke. The scent that followed her mother home on the worst days.

"Well, *wake up*, little girl." Lois breathed at her as she squeezed her face. "Those days of come and go, and do what you like and la-di-da, are *history*. Do you hear me? You've got a lot of responsibility now, and it's time for you to start growing the hell up."

Lois roughly brushed Joanne aside to get to Davey, who quaked like an old washing machine behind her. "Come here, dear," Lois said, and started pulling his hat, mittens, and coat off. He looked at her like she was a stranger on the bus, undressing him like that. Joanne ran as fast as she could, down the hall to her room, and slammed the door.

When Davey gently pushed the door open ten minutes later, Joanne was lying facedown on the bed, with her coat on.

"Joanne?" he whispered. She didn't say anything. "Joanne?" He was the kind of kid who would stand there and say her name a hundred times, assuming she hadn't heard him. "Joanne?"

"Go away, Davey." She sobbed into the pillow.

He stood for a few seconds, looking at her, then looking at the door thinking he might leave, then looking at her some more. Then, as if he'd never called her name before, or he forgot that he had, or maybe he wanted to talk even though she told him not to, he called her low again.

"Jo? Joey? Okay, well, I had, okay, the best time today that I ever had before, is all, Jo. Okay?" He backed out of the room when she didn't lift her face. "Okay? Joey. Bye I'll leave you alone now, Jo."

SUMPIN' NICE

People always spoke to Davey like he was a baby. They did it when he was a baby, did it when he was no longer a baby. Some people never stopped talking to him that way. Davey's mother Lois was the one who set the tone. She didn't mean anything by it, had always spoken to her other children that way when they were small ones. This time around, though, it was just one more thing she couldn't quite snap out of.

"You wan' me bring you back sumpin' nice, sweetie?" was Lois's standard refrain whenever she would leave the house without him. She never left him as an infant, unless five-year-old Joanne was there to take care of him. But later, when Davey was a big lump of a four- and five-year-old and Lois was running low on the patience, physical strength, and unflinching devotion it took to keep hauling him in and out of the car, to the grocery store, to the bank, to the mall, to stop at bathrooms, to answer his questions, to eat at the "family" restaurants she was damn sick of, she began to slip.

Without consistent adult companionship for slightly more than the duration of Davey's life, Lois was more and more anxious to be shed of the boy for whatever minutes she could carve out of a day. The checks always set her off, the child support that sometimes came in the mail from Sneaky Pete, and sometimes didn't, and sometimes came in at three times the amount he was supposed to send if Old Pete had a particularly good run of luck at Hialeah. The money, though it didn't last long, got the itch going for Lois as soon as the mailman arrived.

First, she started leaving Davey in the car for the two minutes it took to punch up the automatic teller machine. Davey didn't mind that. He was that kind of kid, that a few minutes of staring out the landau window at passing cars and pedestrians was not an unpleasant thing. That worked out well enough that the money from the machine could be spent during a fifteen-minute spin through CVS without it hurting the boy much, as long as the doors were locked, and a juice box was within Davey's reach.

Lois loved Davey through it all. When she broke out in a sweat at the checkout counter and made a frantic dash back to the car, sometimes leaving every item unbought on the counter, it was because she could see his face. She could feel, actually feel, the throbbing of his little boy's heart in her own racing, palpitating heart. "Never, never, *never*, never again, sweetheart," Lois promised as she squeezed him, hugging him close to her without removing his seatbelt, making him groan and grip his juice box so hard it gunned apple juice all over the car windows. He smiled and hugged back, though he didn't understand the fuss.

She *did*, did love him. Only she wasn't very good at it anymore. She was a grown woman, lonely, and very weak, she knew. Just for a minute, or maybe ten or twenty, she had to make her little escape and find out, after all these years, who she was, what *she* was thinking, to hear the sound of her own voice and not the sound of her mother's coming out of her mouth and ricocheting around the walls, off the dirty dishes, into the cavernous empty refrigerator.

The problem was that it got easier. When fifteen minutes, and then forty-five, didn't seem to faze the unflappable, serene Davey, it seemed okay to leave him in the house—which was after all much more secure—during those same errands.

"I bring you back sumpin' nice, Davey, okay?" Lois would say as she held Davey's cheeks between her hands. And she always did bring him something. Usually candy or a whole small pizza which she told him he didn't have to share with her or with Joanne when she came home from school. He adored pizza and he adored having things of his own, having things he was in charge of, and Lois reveled in sitting quietly on the couch as he ate it all up in front of the TV.

When Joanne came home from school, Davey proudly showed her the empty box, which he'd always save to show off. Joanne pretended to be jealous, then took him into the kitchen for their daily macaroni and cheese, which he would eat no matter what else he had in his belly. And she made sure to glare defiantly at her mother, knowing by now what the pizza box meant. Lois would not acknowledge the look, and snapped at Joanne to remember not to leave her brother alone which she was out. The more Lois herself left him, the more insistent she would be that Joanne *stay* with him.

To fill the days before Joanne came home, hours that she knew were getting longer and longer for Lois, Joanne started picking things up for Davey at junk shops and yard sales. She bought him Chutes and Ladders, which he played by himself and never cheated at. She bought him as many G.I. Joe dolls and Matchbox cars as she could afford with her own, irreg- ular, secret, Sneaky Pete monies that came addressed to her. She bought him an Etch-A-Sketch, which for some reason had a bald spot in the middle where you could not get the magnetic sand to stick so Davey had to draw everything with a big donut hole in the middle of it.

Davey was interested in everything and he worshipped Joanne, so that every little gift, every broken-down something that somebody didn't want (Joanne was not above picking a thing out of the trash on her way to school and carrying it around with her all day if she thought it would be good for her brother), turned out to be something he loved. But he somehow couldn't manage to love anything for long. Not that he didn't appreciate it, he just couldn't sustain anything. One day a game was the most important thing in his world, the next it was just one more decoration on the carpet, strewn around him with everything else as he returned to the thrall of the TV screen.

Until Joanne brought home Operation, the game where you get to play surgeon, pulling body parts out of a patient with a pair of electrified tweezers. Unlike most of his toys, Operation worked perfectly. From the first time Davey accidentally touched the side trying to remove the funny bone, and the big red nose flashed along with the alarming buzzer to tell him—shock him, actually—that he had failed, he was hooked. He kept Operation by his side as he watched TV and dutifully went to work saving the patient's life during commercials. Sometimes during boring shows that he only watched because nothing else was on, like *All My Children*, he would even operate while the program was on.

Joanne loved to see him react like that. Lois was pleased

that he'd found an interest, one that seemed to have captured his imagination and that he could take in the car with him. But Operation began to consume Davey's time much the same way television had, to the point where he sometimes wouldn't back off the game for hours at a time except to shake his operating hand in a writer's-cramp-type shake. After a while it started to bother Joanne, though Lois didn't seem to mind.

"How you doin'?" Joanne said as she walked in from school. As soon as she spoke she heard the familiar, annoying, mocking *buzzzz!* of failure.

"I *killed* him," Davey roared as he swung his face in her direction. "*Again*, I killed him. Like before and like before." He was sitting at the kitchen table, kneeling on his chair actually. Just as he had been when Joanne left in the morning.

"No TV, Davey?" she said.

He shook his head "no" as gently as he could because he was trying to remove the patient's heart. But it was not gently enough, as the buzz returned. "*Dead*, he's dead. I killed him dead," Davey said as he slapped his palm on the table.

"Where's Ma?" Joanne asked.

Davey simply stared at the dead patient, took the tweezers in his fist and started hammering himself, jabbing the tweezers into his thigh again and again.

"Stop that," Joanne yelled, grabbing his hand. Finally he looked at her. "Where is Ma?" she said slowly.

"I don't know," he said. "She went to the store. I don't know." He pulled the tweezers back from her and resumed work, immediately setting off the buzzer. It was then Joanne noticed that, despite the hours and hours of playing, he wasn't getting any better at it. He *was* intense, and committed, that was for sure. But his hand had this little tremble, something no one could have ever noticed before, that would not allow him to remove any but the easiest pieces without stumbling. Through sheer force of will he managed to extract the heart once in every ten tries, but the rest was all frustration, and now fury.

Lois came sweeping through the door. She would not look at Joanne. This was the first time Lois had left Davey alone and not returned before Joanne came home.

"Sumpin' *extra* special today, Davey," she said, with a lot of extra gush. She pulled from a sandwich-sized brown paper bag an extra-large Milky Way bar. Davey took it with a smile. Then slowly, dramatically, she pulled out a bottle, short, curvy, green. A seven-ounce Coca-Cola bottle.

The candy bar fell right out of Davey's hand. He snatched the bottle out of Lois's hand and stared into it, like into a microscope.

"Great, huh, Davey," Lois gushed. "They just reissued them, the old-style bottles. The ones you loved. Isn't that nice? Do you remember, Davey?"

He remembered, of course, because the last time he'd drunk from one was only two months before. Just before his grandmother died. Gram, Lois's mother, was the one who always brought around the old Cokes—not the reissues—from some secret stash she kept in the dirt cellar of the house she grew up in herself, raised Lois in, and eventually died in. She said she knew of places, some secret network of distributors and collectors all as nutty as she was, who would refill and reuse the old thick scratchy bottles. Yet once in a while Davey downed one that was clearly an original out of Gram's private stock, flat syrupy contents and all. Those he loved best.

Gram, who didn't like her daughter, never spoke to her, and never entered her house even though they lived within walking distance of each other, would come by like an apparition, like some all-knowing silent spirit as soon as Lois left on summer mornings. She would turn the corner and walk up to find, inevitably, Davey perched on the top step, working up the first beads of sweat on any one of a million long, long summer days. Those days when Davey just sat around, quietly crazy with the sticky dead heat and cicada buzzing high and loud right at him to warn him that tomorrow was going to be nothing but the same all over again. He sat on that porch for hours and hours, staring into his jar of beetles and bees—more often than not hunted and retrieved for him by Joanne—and shaking the jar now and then to make them fight. Maybe once or twice a day Lois would come by on her way to somewhere or back and pat him on top of his fuzzy head like a good, quiet watchdog.

But Gram would appear in one of those housedresses with flowers like wallpaper that seem to be made just for old people. She brought with her, whether it was ten a.m. or ten p.m., the bottle of Coke and a tiny bag of cheese curls. Cheesy Weesies, is what she called them, something Davey never heard anyone else say, and which always made him feel silly when he heard it even though he was not a silly boy. The old woman and the little boy wouldn't share ten words the whole time, as she sat and he consumed, but it was like a brief friendship, some kind of mutually knowing relationship, packed into the few minutes it took him to polish it all off. Gram always waited until Davey was done, took her bottle back, and was off again.

No one knew what the deal was between Davey and Gram—all they could do was watch. If Lois happened to stumble across them in her comings and goings, she would just continue on her way, the three of them wordless and flat as if Lois were a mere tumbleweed blowing by.

So no one knew, never even thought about it, when the day of Gram's funeral Davey sat it out, in his perch on the porch, the whole day. Staring into space as guests came and went, patting him on the head as they passed. Through all the visits, all come, all gone, Davey sat largely unnoticed even though he was not a little boy anymore but a big beanstalk of a kid who came to people's waists even when he was sitting. Waiting on the porch as if it were July and not November. It was suppertime and bitter freezing black under the broken porch light before Lois figured it all out and hauled him, stiff and reluctant and still staring, inside.

He was still staring into his grandmother's bottle, or his jar of bees, when Lois interrupted him. "Now isn't *that* sumpin' nice," she said into Davey's ear from over his shoulder. She was trying hard, but she just didn't know. "Open it," she said, rushing to the utility drawer and pulling out an opener. "None of that twist-off stuff with *this*." She was sure, once more, that the magic was in the bottle.

Davey looked at her for only a second. He put the bottle down with a bump, picked up the tweezers, and starting playing Operation more maniacally than ever. His hand shook spastically, setting off the buzzer again and again until it became an almost unbroken line of buzz. But he continued on, as if he were doing it on purpose.

"I can't *stand* that sound anymore!" Joanne yelled. She yelled not at Davey, but at Lois. Joanne stared at Lois, who stood with a wounded, confused face looking down at Davey, who stared at Operation.

Finally Joanne stormed off to her room, nothing but the electronic game noise, the failure alarm, behind her. That sound hung in her head all night as she tried to sleep. It sounded, after a while, just like the cicada buzz chasing her in the summer heat.

In the morning, before anyone woke up, Joanne pried the back panel off the Operation game and snipped every wire she could find with her nail clippers. She carefully replaced the panel and went back to bed.

When she came home from school that afternoon, Joanna found the game had joined the rest of the discarded games on the floor in front of the TV, and Davey was glued to cartoons. She dropped her coat, went up to him from behind and sat. They sat together flat bottomed on the floor, Joanne's legs running out alongside his, her arms wrapped around him, hands clasped over his chest.

"Sorry, Dave," she said. He nodded without turning, though he hadn't a clue. Joanne had started the whole Operation thing without asking him, and had ended it the same way. She *was* sorry. But as he leaned back and settled into her, she also felt a little rush of power, of control over the chaos that was this house. That she *wasn't* sorry for.

LIKE A BIRD OUT OF WATER

But I hardly ever see him anyway my dad is the one who changes me more than anybody else can change me and I don't know why 'cause he really doesn't know me very well or at least I don't know him.

His name is Pete. Sneaky Pete is what my mother calls him and I guess that's true enough since he shows up without telling anybody and without permission even though he's supposed to have some kind of permission if he wants to come and see me and Jo. But he doesn't bother anybody and he's always gone by the time Ma comes home since he always knows when to come when she's not here. He never does anything bad to us kids or to Ma neither and in fact leaves us all presents including perfume for Ma so I think the thing is not so much that he's here that makes her so mean but that he isn't here.

Now you take good care of Ol' Lois for me, okay, son? he says every single time I see him. Life and me ain't been all too kind to your poor ma, but I still love her and wouldn't want nothin' to ever harm her. And she's very harmable, you know.

So is what I say because I can't think of any reason not to say it. Why don't you stay here and take care of her yourself and take care of everybody else while you're at it? And Sneaky Pete laughs and plays with his gray whiskers with his long long fingers that wear all the giant gold rings with horns and skulls and goats and the one pinky ring with the coin in the middle of it. He's real skinny and the rings slide up and down his fingers and he twirls them and turns them right all the time when he talks.

Because I can't is about all he can tell me. I can't take care of Lois and she can't take care of me, so all we can do is cross our fingers and hope that somebody we love is going to look after both of us. And the way I see it Davey, that somebody around here should be you. Look at you, you big strappin' sonofabitch. You must be a foot taller than your old man already.

Made me feel big every time he came around. Not so much the thing about the tallness since I'm a foot taller than pretty much *everybody* since last year but the whole man thing and he said the things he said in a soft voice like a flute only deeper. Don't listen to him don't look in his eagle eyes for more than a second was what Ma always told me because that nasty old Sneaky Pete is a snake charmer who knows what each and every person needs to hear and he tells it to them like a song. But then she cries when I tell her that he was here when she wasn't.

He knew about *me* that much was for true. He gave me my bike which after everything changed me more than anything. It gave me the other kind of me the one I like better. There's the kind of me that stays home or sits in school and doesn't say much out loud but goes on and on in here in the head without even stopping for a single little mental breath. The kind of me that makes me nervous. The kind of me that makes me feel like a fish in the sky trying to fly or a bird in the water. Only the other kind of me the one that I think Dad knew about somehow I don't know how but after all he's Sneaky Pete who knows everything so that's how he knew but the kind of me that I can be on the bike. That talks a whole different way and doesn't have the heavy beating heart that anyone can see thumping in my bony chest if I ever take my shirt off in front of people which so I never do. But instead the me that works perfectly in rhythm with the oily *ch-ch-ch* of the eighteen-speed tiger-paw mountain bike that takes me as far as I want over all and every terrain snow rocks curb or mud with no problem in total control. It's a control machine.

I can't hardly say three straight words out loud because of the so many millions I got flying around inside playing like a racquetball game in my skull so loud and so fast and so every which direction at once that I can't even try to talk over it. Like no one word or thought is more or less important than the others so there ain't no order and they all just climb over each other to get out all at the same time. And the more all happens to me inside the less I can say it out. The bike though the bike makes it all work like shifting gears and pushing the pedals left right left right and before you know it I'm where I want to be doing what I want to do and it makes a lot more sense and is a lot quieter.

Nothing like exercise for the head, boy, Sneaky Pete said like he knew all about my head when he wheeled the bike into my bedroom last time. Middle of the night like spook Santa Claus he came in and left it right there against the footboard kissed me on the ear and was gone again before I was even through twisting the sleeps out of my eyes. And Gary says hi, he said as he slipped away. Gary's my brother who ran away to live with Dad and then hit some old woman in the head because she had something he wanted and who now lives in jail and who we never hear from which is okay with me.

He's a great guy my dad. He lives in Florida.

LOVE, SISTER, IT'S JUST A KISS AWAY

There were just those days. Those days when she quit and ran and didn't care much what it looked like to the neighbors or to Joanne or to any damn body else who wanted to look at what Lois was doing with herself and her responsibilities. Flight. Was all.

And usually Davey was no trouble, no trouble to nobody. That was Davey. "Okay Davey" Joanne would call him, practically spitting it in his face when she saw him sitting for it, just taking and taking and taking whatever crap it was that Lois dished up on him. Lois was peeling out again, leaving Davey, all five years of him, in a cloud of her dust. "I'm going out now, Davey," Lois said. "Okay," Davey said. "Make yourself a sandwich for supper," Lois said. "Okay," Davey said.

Joanne opened up Davey's supper sandwich, which sat

on the table long after their mother had returned. She'd told him to make the sandwich, but eating it was his own option. Lois remained barricaded in her room, talking on the phone, alternately giggling like a schoolgirl and crying like a Siamese cat, after a long afternoon out *there*. The sandwich Davey made for himself had one slice of bologna in it, dry. "Okay Davey, Okay Davey," Joanne snapped at him as she flung the sandwich in the bucket. "You don't have to just sit there and *take* everything, y'know, Davey. If you want a decent supper, then you can say something else besides 'okay.'"

"What should I say, Jo?"

Joanne walked up and pinched Davey's lean upper arm, twisting as much flesh as she could grip between her thumb and fingernails. "Wake up," she yelled. "Snap out of it, will you? Wake up."

He didn't acknowledge any pain. "Is that what I should say?" he asked placidly.

Lois came out of her room and walked toward the kitchen. All conversation stopped as Joanne walked first to the refrigerator, then to the stove, and started scrambling an egg for Davey.

The next day, as Lois was leaving, Joanne's words still hung in Davey's head. "Where are you goin'?" Davey shocked his mother, as if his were a strange voice coming out of the walls rather than out of the little boy who sat cross-legged on the living-room rug. She dropped her pocketbook on the bare floor by the front door, sending keys, makeup, change, Doublemint gum, and Salem cigarettes scattering across the hardwood. She crouched down to collect it in her waist-length rabbit coat, and Davey scurried over to help her.

He asked her again, as they stooped nose to nose, "Where are you goin'?"

It was another one of those days. "I'm goin' where the action is," she said.

"Will you take me with you?" he said.

Again Lois was stunned, but this time not scared. Her stomach was fluttery with confusion, with a gentle spark of weird warm excitement, as she looked into the bottomless-ness of Davey's pale green eyes. Like a girl, like she'd been waiting so long, and she'd finally been asked to get up and dance.

She did so love Davey, as much as she could.

"It's really nice there, Davey. It really is a nice place, so many nice people, and fun."

"I wanna buy my man here a ginger ale, Victor," Lois said as she first gave Davey a boost onto the corner bar stool, then took the one next to him. Davey shied from the big neon Löwenbräu sign that blinked off and on beside him face.

"You got it, babe," Victor said as he pulled out the black

mini garden hose and squirted a glass full. Then he yanked the cap off a long-neck Budweiser and slid it to Lois without her asking. "Oh," she said, sounding as if she were surprised by the thought of paying. She started pawing clumsily around her purse.

"Don't worry about it, sweetheart," Victor said, reaching over the bar and patting her hand. "It's all right."

"You see, I told you, Davey. There are just the nicest people here," Lois said. "Victor here is the best of the lot, of course, but there are some pretty powerful figures like to hang out here as well. This is the kind of place, Davey, where a person could meet big lawyers, who come in from the courthouse right down the block, or city officials, they like to come here too, or doctors, Davey, a lot of doctors like to come in here from the city hospital because it's right next door practically. Exciting, don'tcha think?" Lois leaned sideways to hug Davey close for a second, and Davey nearly slipped off the stool leaning into her.

"Yo, Lo, how 'bout a go?" asked a tall skinny man with a black ski hat resting way up on the crown of his head. He had a stubble and a salt-and-pepper mustache that grew down over his lip like a walrus's. As he spoke he dangled two wiggling fingers, like tiny legs dancing.

"Oh, I don't know, Jerome. I'm gonna have to ask my escort here if it's all right."

"Oh, whoo whoo," Jerome laughed. "I didn't even see the little feller."

"Davey, can I? Do you mind?" Lois said. She thought all this was cute, as she held his hand between her two, pleading. But her mind was already on the dance floor, where Willie Nelson's voice was filling the place with "Blue Eyes Crying in the Rain." "Oh, thank you, sweetie," she said as she kissed his cheek, even though his only response had been to make his eyes even bigger and wider than usual.

As Lois led the way out to the dance floor, Jerome leaned into Davey, getting right up close to his face with a red-eyed grin. "We just might have to take this outside, pard-ner," Jerome said, making two bony fists and shaking them theatrically beside his cheeks. Lois had turned to watch, and was laughing, thinking it was great fun all around, not notic-ing how Davey was pulling farther and farther back from Jerome, into the Löwenbräu sign, turning rigid with fear. She just never saw it. She'd lost the thread again.

Victor leaned out over the bar, *way* over this time. He reached out and with his great big hand grabbed Jerome's entire face. He squeezed that face like he was palming a soft-ball as he talked.

"It's not funny," Victor growled before he pushed Jerome's head straight back, sending him stumbling toward the dance floor. Lois took Jerome's hand as he started pulling her along.

Now she looked a bit concerned. "I'll be right back, Davey," she called. "Now, Vic, you take care of my boy while I'm gone. Anything he wants, understand. He's the king." And she was gone, bobbing in the small sea of gently rotating bodies.

Victor put his hands flat on the bar and looked at Davey, sizing him up. Davey stared likewise back.

"I like your mother, kid. She's a good egg. Everybody likes her. But y'know, what's not to like, right? She don't make no trouble, she don't drink too much, she's sweet as pie to everybody else. She, y'know, she brightens up the place."

Davey didn't say anything, didn't nod, didn't grunt. Just did the round-eye, exaggerated in the flashing and unflashing neon.

"But I don't know really about who she's gonna meet in here, y'know the politicians and doctors and all that. I mean, we got 'em, a course, but they ain't what you'd call the grade-A kind if you know what I mean. Hacks, Flacks, and Quacks, is what I like to call 'em. Y'know, mostly just a batch of bulbous broke-downs that have been at what they been at for way on too long." He paused for some kind of reaction from Davey that simply wasn't forthcoming. "But good people. A course. All good people."

Victor was called to the other end of the bar by an enormous balding woman in a sweatsuit banging her glass on the bar repeatedly like a baby with a spoon. Davey turned to try to find his mother dancing. He scanned the crowd, mentally sorting through the men, so many of whom looked like Jerome but were not dancing with his mother. Davey shifted from one hip to the other, then back, craning his neck to pick her out, as one slow country ballad melted away in a cry of steel guitar and another rose up. But the bodies kept moving as one, everybody, it seemed, rubbing against each other, and rubbing and rubbing, and he couldn't exactly pick Lois out of it. He thought he saw her whiter-than-the-rest face peek out, thought he saw the red light catch her burned permed hair. But maybe not.

Victor threw a bag of potato chips on the bar, the crackle catching Davey's attention. "But you don't need to be bothered by none of all that, about what's wrong with everybody who comes in here, now do ya?" He turned and ripped the cellophane off a six-inch pepperoni pizza, threw it like a Frisbee into a toaster oven, and slammed the door. "You're just a kid, right?"

Davey opened the bag of oily chips and bore down on it, finishing it off in about a minute.

"Wow," Victor said, stepping back, folding his arms across the barrel chest, and nodding. The bell rang on the toaster oven. He turned and pulled the pizza out, flung it quickly, because it was sizzling hot, onto a plate that already had crumbs on it. He yelled, "Mimi," then sailed the plate down the bar, where it was intercepted by the waitress who, with her black mop, skeletal face, and mole looked just like Abraham Lincoln.

"What more should I give you now?" he said, half to himself since he wasn't expecting answers from Davey at this point. He grabbed a bag of honey-roasted peanuts off the Eagle Snacks rack above the beer chest. "I'm sorry," Victor said, and he meant it. "But I don't know too much about no kids, kid. But you should like peanuts, huh? And they got honey on 'em. Sugar, sweet stuff, y'know." Victor ripped down a second bag, to read the ingredients. "Ya, kid, this should be okay. You should like this."

He watched with pleasure as Davey wolfed down the peanuts. The fourth sad song since Lois left started playing. Jim Reeves singing "Then You Can Tell Me Good-bye." "But like I say anyways, I don't know nothin' 'bout no kids. How old are you anyway, kid? Like, I dunno, ten or somethin'?"

Davey crumpled the foil bag in his left hand, looked up at Victor, and held up his five fingers on his right hand.

"Ouch," Victor said. "You're *five*? Boy was I off, huh? But I told you I don't know nothin' about it, kid. But whoa, maybe you shouldn't be in here?" He started talking to himself again. "Nah, it's okay. This ain't that kinda place. We got your pizzas and your booths and your hot dogs, buffalo wings, 'tater skins. This is a restaurant. Ain't like it's a bar, it's a restaurant, right, kid?"

"Davey."

Now it was Victor's turn to give the wide-eyed stare. "Excuse me?"

"Davey. You call me kid, but my name is Davey. You heard, back before, my mom call me Davey, but you call me kid. I like Davey better, please."

"You're absolutely right, little monk," said Victor, bowing at the waist. While he still couldn't get a smile, or any real facial expression out of the boy, Victor got closer, elbows on the bar. Davey didn't pull away from Victor, but looked right back at him. "I'll tell you this, Davey: I might not know nothin' about kids, but I know this much." Victor could not take his eyes off Davey's eyes, Davey's big, sea-glass green, sea-glass murky, unblinking eyes. "You're an *old* kid. Ain't ya, Davey?"

"Vic, Vic," a customer called.

"Be right witcha, Davey," Victor said as he went to serve.

Davey slid off the bar stool and walked to the dance floor to catch up with his mother. First he stood at the edge of the floor, looking up at the twenty or so couples dancing slow, tight together, everybody looking so unusually tall, plus the extra four inches added by the raised dancing area. But nobody on that side was Lois. Davey started wading in. Nobody seemed to notice him. He took a light elbow to the head from a plump, happy-faced woman, somebody else's mother, who looked down and said, "Oohh my oh my, innee cute." He bounced like a bumper car from one hip to another as people went about their romance as if there was no little person pushing his way through, stopping to stare up at every woman. At the very center of the throng, Davey stood momentarily frozen, being bumped again and again by the same two men, who had him sandwiched between their rear ends. He lost track of which direction was the one he came from and which was the one he wanted. The bodies hitting him were like black trees closing in beside him and over him until the air seemed to be getting hotter in Davey's lungs, and easier to taste on the way down. "Get along now, darlin'," a woman said, not too friendly, as she gave Davey a little shove toward the back wall of the room. The far end of the dance floor.

Which was where, coming to a small clearing, Davey found Lois. She had gone to the farthest spot from where she had left Davey, just looking for that little bit of privacy, for those few minutes, for herself and for Davey too. She and Jerome were dancing in a private space between two cabaret tables against the wall, with a distance of no more than three feet between them and the other dancers. But with the others so packed together, it was like their own little stage. Davey stood and watched. Because he couldn't do anything else.

He watched as Jerome kissed his mother on the neck, up

and down her neck, working one side and then the other. Lois closed her eyes and threw her head back. They continued to dance, more slowly than the others. Jerome nibbled her neck, nibbled her earlobe, took a nip off her chin. Lois started kissing him back. Jerome's back was to Davey, and Davey could see the top half of her face as she waggled her head in one direction, Jerome in the other. Trying to swallow each other in their mating dance. Like spiders. Their feet moved almost too slowly for the eye to see by the time they had rotated to where Lois's back was to her son. Davey watched Jerome's hands. Stained with something like dirty motor oil, those hands slid up and down and up Lois's sides. Then down again, his hands slid. Down, Davey watched, over his mother's backside, up and down again, rubbing it with both hands, feeling it, then squeezing it, kneading it, squeezing his mother's behind as she swiveled her hips to accommodate.

The song ended. Lois opened her eyes and started talking, nuzzling into Jerome's face. Davey walked backward, back into the crowd. He banged into a man who grabbed him by the shoulders, spun him around, and sent him on his way. A new song came up, something jumpier this time, with fiddle and accordion, and the dancers started bopping. This time they jostled Davey all around. He found his face momentarily pressed into the soft inviting hip of a woman, and almost nuzzled it, almost embraced it, almost held on and hugged.

Next thing, though, the hip stuck out and bumped him off, on his way again. Sharper elbows jabbing his head, pointy cowboy boots cracking his ankles. But none of it felt like crisp, bone-on-bone blows to Davey. They were just bumps, knocking him almost off his feet, the impact somehow muffled. As if he was wearing a lot of sweaters, a lot of thick heavy socks, a leather boxing helmet.

Davey's eyes were swollen as he climbed back on the stool. He stared at the polished surface of the bar.

"Hey, I missed ya, little monk," Victor said. "Thought maybe you wasn't comin' back." Davey didn't look up. Victor stooped to look up into his face. "Glad ya *did*, though," he said.

"Well hey there, big man," Lois said, her hands on Davey's shoulders. Jerome was not with her. Davey looked up as she sat down next to him and showed her the exact placid face he had on before she left. "Old Vic takin' care of you?" she said.

Davey looked at Vic, who smiled proudly at the job he'd done. "Ya, he is," Davey said. Vic flipped him another bag of honey roasts, which Davey devoured like the others.

"I'm gonna go home now, Ma," Davey said, wiping a grain of salt from the corner of his mouth with one finger.

"Really, Davey?" she said, trying to sound more disappointed than guilty.

"Ya, Ma, I'm ready."

"Okay, we'll go then, I guess."

"No. You don't have to go, I know the way. It's only a little ways. I *want* you to stay, really."

Lois paused, then took Davey's hand. She turned and stared at Victor for a few seconds until he walked away, shaking his head. "Are you sure, Davey? 'Cause I'll go with you, if you want."

He shook his head as he hopped down. "No, Ma, I want you to stay."

From the far end of the bar, Victor waved to Davey. Davey stopped in the doorway and waved back.

"I'll be right along, honey," Lois called extra loudly. "I'll be *right* there. Tell your sister I'll be right along."

Davey nodded and pushed the door open, letting the last of the daylight come in and slice the bar down the middle. Then he closed the door quietly behind him.

DECKED OUT IN CHEESE

Sneaky Pete could do this trick where he extended his right arm, straight out from the shoulder, shift, align, maneuver it just so, so that the elbow joint dislocated and the arm fell swinging as if it were the pendulum of a morbid grandfather clock. Like the arm of a dead thing, with no bone in it at all, the limb hung there with all the big gold rings pulling the lifeless hand toward the floor. Sneaky Pete looked at it smiling, admiring it like it was a show he was watching along with everybody else rather than a part of his own body. Cigarette stuck to his bottom lip, riding up and down as he spoke and up and down, but never falling out.

"Don't try this at home now, younguns." Pete laughed. "I once did this for a group of sailors and one of them tried it . . . never got the damn thing back into the socket."

Davey was already trying it, his arm thrust straight out. Joanne slapped the arm down. Pete went to the refrigerator and pulled out a half-bottle of sangria that had a balled-up napkin stuck in it, supposedly to keep it fresh. He walked back into the living room, taking a long pull on the bottle as he moved.

"So where's Lois?" he asked, wiping his mouth with his palm.

Davey shrugged.

"I don't know," Joanne said. "But I'm not worried. She'll come back. She always does." She sighed when she said the last part, and said it as if it wasn't necessarily a good thing.

"Jesus damn," Pete said. "The woman still hasn't got a brain in her bleedin' head."

Davey pulled back when he heard Pete talking like that. Pete noticed. "I'm sorry, guys. Don't get me wrong. I love your mother to hell, I really do. It's just that she can be such an asshole."

Joanne nodded, knowingly, maturely. The nod that often earned her a slap from her mother. She liked it when Sneaky Pete snuck in, because she loved talking and listening to him, and showing him how mature she was now that she was twelve.

Davey didn't like it so much. Not that he didn't like Pete's appearances, his mysterious, exciting arrivals that came in bunches several times a year when he came up north to go to Saratoga, or the Belmont, the Budweiser Million, or Mass Cap. Four times Lois had changed the lock and four times had screamed at finding Pete strolling through the door like there was no door. What Davey didn't like was he couldn't listen to anybody run his mother down. Even Joanne knew that if she wanted to bad-mouth Lois with Davey in earshot, she was probably going to have to duke it out with her brother.

Davey turned away from Pete and inched his way up to point-blank range on the TV. Then he cranked the volume. Pete silently walked to the coffee table and picked up the remote. He clicked off the TV and drained the wine bottle at the same time.

"Road Trip," Pete sang.

"Yee-hah," Joanne yelled.

"Where are we going?" Davey asked, but hopped to his feet before he got his answer. Pete held out his hand from across the room. Davey came and held it.

"We're going where the action is," Sneaky Pete said, nodding.

"Your mother ever tell you about how we met, about the guy I blinded?" Pete said as the three of them strolled hand in hand down the middle of the midway. Davey was half listening as he looked hard at every vendor, every game hawker they passed. The cotton-candy spinner, the noisy air rifles with the bent barrels. Saucer-eyed Davey, the candy-colored carnival lights glinting off those big impossible eyes, was too much to resist for the carnies. Every oily slickmaster with a dirty apron on looked right at Davey when he passed.

"C'mere, boy, first three for free. See how easy it is?"

"Have a dart, cow eyes. Letcha throw one for nothin'. An' the rest's only three a quarter."

"*Evv*erybody a winner! A winner *evv*ery time," said the skeletal woman running the floating ducks game, waving Davey toward her with both hands. "Ooohh, sweetie, you're too cute to lose. Come aaaaaahhn."

Davey held tight to Pete's hand, never changed expression though he was repulsed and entranced by every come-on.

"I don't know that I actually *blinded* the guy, mind you," Pete said. "But I think so. Lois never told you guys about this, huh?"

"No, she stinks with stories," Joanne said, tugging playfully at Pete's hand. "You tell it, Dad. Go on."

"All right, all right, but first let's get some nourishment." Sneaky Pete stepped up to the concession stand, where the black-haired teenage boy who served them looked like he'd been dipping his long sad face into the fryolator.

"Cotton candy," Joanne said.

"Excellent choice, Jo. Cotton is the all-natural fabric, good for you. Davey? Whadya say, dude? Fried dough? Sausage?"

Davey continued to stare at the amusements. He turned to his father and shrugged.

"Two fried doughs and one cotton candy," Pete said to the kid, who turned, slammed a few big utensils, whipped a big stick around in the pink swirl of grainy sugary fiberglass, and pulled a hissing metal basket out of the hot oil.

"Six bucks," the kid said as he leaned over the counter. As he hung there, he looked down at Davey, who was looking up. The kid fixed him with a cold, lifeless stare, and Davey responded with a warm, lifeless stare. As they walked away Davey continued to look back at the kid, who didn't move. He just stayed there draped over the counter because he had no other customers and there was no reason not to.

Davey and Joanne sat on either side of Pete, on the patchy brown grass in front of a trailer.

"It was at a carnival just like this one," Pete began, powdered sugar dusting his mustache. "But then again all carnivals are just like this one, ain't they? But it was right over here that it happened, behind all the trailers. See, Lois was at the show with this big ol' Harley cat, tall more than anything. Tell ya the truth, he was more leather than muscle anyway. So I starts to makin' the old eyes at your ma and she of course starts to makin' 'em at me and ol' stupid Harley finally, finally gets wind of it and we gotta go out back."

Davey's head was toggling back, and forth, between listening to Pete's story and watching the carnival patrons walk by with their giant inflatable crayons and their dancing monkeys on a stick and their Lynyrd Skynyrd smoked-glass mirrors. Joanne listened closely to every breath her father took.

"Thing is, this guy is a carny, working that very carnival sometimes, so we attract a big crowd. Every geek who could slip away from his booth is there watching the fight. But the fight doesn't last long. The guy picks me up, right up in the air—he's a strong wiry sonofabitch after all—and starts to squeezin' holy hell out of my gutwork. So I do the only thing I can. I take these"—Pete held two thumbs up—"and I give the guy two thumbdogs, *jammin'* the suckers so hard into his eyeballs that the thumbs sink in, right on up to the knuckles."

Joanne dropped her cotton candy and covered her mouth with both hands. But she leaned even harder into Sneaky Pete, and her dancing eyes showed more excitement than horror. Davey stopped looking everywhere else and turned his attention strictly on Pete.

Sneaky Pete shivered his shoulders. "You know what it felt like, there at the ends of my thumbs? It felt like . . . I dunno, eyeballs, I guess. Wet and warm and hard but not hard. Felt like I was thumbing hard-boiled eggs. Twenty-minute eggs. Only they were alive things, and felt it."

"What about Ma, what did Ma do?" Joanne said, brushing the dirt off her cotton candy.

Sneaky Pete tipped his head back, looking up to the sky. "Lois," he said softly. "She was a fine thing, your mother. Red leather skirt, legs up to here, cut-off T-shirt, suede vest. Kids, I want you to know, your mother was like some kinda queen back then. And you know what she did? She did the right thing. She left with me, of course. But first she walked right on over to that Harley boy, who had fallen like a tree on his back, and lay still like one, she crouched down to him and she kissed him. Stuff oozing outta his eyes and everything, and Lois kisses the sucker. Gallant is what ol' Lo was back then. Is that what they call it, for girls? Gallant? Anyway, she left with me then. It was a very Romeo and Juliet kind of thing, y'know?"

"And the other guy, Dad? He was really blind, was he?" You did it to him?" Joanne said, almost breathless.

"Well I don't know for sure, but I don't expect he did much more seein' outta them balls. Hey, I lost a nail in one of 'em. Somebody even told me later the dude croaked, a thumbs in the brain deal or somethin', but I don't believe that. Not that it mattered. He was just a carny loser nobody, a Gypsy. Even when he was lyin' there, nobody did nothin' for him 'cause they all had to get back to their booths. The only thing anybody cared about him at that point was, like, now who's gonna run the water-gun races with him gone? Poor stupid Gypsy nobody."

That was where Davey got off.

"Let's go," Davey suddenly said, jumping to his feet, pulling Pete by the hand. "I don't want to do stories. I want to play games." He started tugging hard.

Joanne stood, brushing herself off. "That's a super story, Dad. A real love story, huh?"

They talked as Davey raced to the baseball pitching game. "It was exactly that, sweetheart. It was a true love story 'cause I knew from the second I laid eyes on her that I was gonna love Lois for the rest of my life. We took off right from that carnival and shot down in my Charger all the way to Atlantic City. Stayed with the Governor. Not the governor in charge of New Jersey, but the governor in charge of pinball machines in New Jersey. Stayed, living like pigs, pigs in love, for two whole weeks."

"Wow, Daddy," Joanne said, jumping on his back. "That's *so* beautiful."

"It was," he said sadly, turning his head so that, with Joanne piggybacking, their cheeks touched. "It was a beautiful time and Lois was a beautiful chick. I ain't never matched her again."

They stepped up behind Davey just as Pete was saying the last words about how wonderful Lois was. Davey spun angrily to face them. He stared at Pete, but Pete didn't get it.

"Kid, you got a friggin' quarter or not? You're in the way."

"Shut up," Pete said, riffing a quarter off the man's chest. "Go ahead, Davey, throw the baseballs."

Davey turned, picked up the baseballs, and threw so wildly that he hit nothing but the stuffed Fred Flintstone dolls on the top shelf. Then he stepped hard on Pete's foot and stalked off. Pete leaned over the counter, with Joanne on his back. He slapped down a five-dollar bill and growled, "Give me Fred friggin' Flintstone."

Pete, carrying Joanne on his back, followed Davey from one rigged game to the next, buying the prizes his son couldn't win. Shooting the paper star target with the air rifle—a stuffed frog. Shooting basketballs—a Miller Lite mug. Throwing the rings around the Coke bottle—a three-foot rubber boa constrictor.

"I love this crap," Sneaky Pete said, breathing deep the smell of old-growth popcorn, sausage, hay, axle grease, perfume, plastic, and sweat. He had the haul of prizes under each arm, his daughter on his back, and Davey slowing down and loosening up to the point where they were all actually traveling together through the show. "Darlin', reach into that pocket there." He pointed with his nose at the breast pocket of his dungaree jacket. Joanne reached in and pulled out a handful of black pills. "Whoa there, you wanna off the old man? Just give me two."

"What are they?" Joanne asked as she placed the pills on her father's lips.

"Blood pressure stuff. Thanks, hon."

"Let's go on the round-up," Joanne said.

"Sure," Pete said. "Come on, Davey."

Davey shook his hand and backed up. Joanne slid down her father's back and pulled Davey along. "Don't be a baby," she said.

"Ya, it'll be fun. It's good to be afraid." Pete laughed.

Davey kept shaking his head, but got on anyway. A minute into the ride, when it reached maximum speed and stood completely vertical spinning like a giant bicycle wheel, Davey vomited. With the motion of the ride, all the throw-up landed on Pete, not Davey, and on the armloads of toys he carried.

Wobbling down the steps of the ride, Davey just wanted to sit. Pete dumped all the stuffed animals in the trash barrel and wiped himself off with five pounds of wet napkins from the hamburger stand. Joanne laughed like a maniac.

All that was left for their efforts were the boa and the beer mug, until Sneaky Pete spotted the cheese jewelry lady. "Hot damn, come on," he whooped. "We're gonna be decked out in cheese," he said, running toward the cluster of little stands on the outer edge of the carnival.

Cheese jewelry was what Pete called the junk—two-dollar watches, wide leather wristbands with metal studs and your name tapped into them, plastic rings with gold paint that cracked off before you reached the car and topped with meatball-sized, diamond-shaped baubles of pink or green— that somehow felt light and fun and trashy carny geek chic on the carnival grounds where the stuff dripped off almost everybody. It was the piece of the evening you wore home to wave in the noses of the tough-luck suckers who couldn't be there. Cheese jewelry was nothing like the stuffed animals, that didn't mean jack after all, because you *wore* it, you *were* it, for a while anyway, the citizen of the carnival, low as it goes.

And though he'd grown into the more pricey kind, cheese jewelry was Sneaky Pete. "Davey, what time is it? No, that's right, you can't tell me because you ain't got a watch." Pete was working up a rev, talking quickly, squeezing the kids' shoulders every few seconds, pointing at one piece of cheese after another. "Sweet Cheeks," he said to the woman with the sunken eyes and the high rouge cheeks. "Lemme have that watch there, will ya?" She pulled down from the wall behind her a watch with a big face and bullets for numerals. "Like it, Davey? Great." He strapped it on Davey's wrist then spun to scope out some more. "But what if it breaks? Can't have my boy not knowin' what time it is. Gimme that one, and that one and that one." He strapped three more on Davey's arm, covering it halfway to the elbow. Davey stared down at them, then back up at Pete with a small, brief smile. "Thanks, Dad," he said, then started setting the time on all of them. "Whadya, want the kid to tip over?" Pete said to the woman. "Gimme four for the other arm." Davey looked like a gladiator.

"Um, excuse me?" Joanne said. Pete scooped her up like a child half her age, and from her position on his hip she went about picking the gaudiest, silliest pieces she could find.

Something else had already caught Davey's eye, and he drifted off. While Sneaky Pete covered his daughter's ears, wrists and fingers with spangles, Davey pulled up a seat at a kiosk called The Temporary Tattooist. Stencil on, color in, not quite as temporary as the Cracker Jack kind of tattoo, but still only something to wear for a couple of weeks instead of forever like the ones on Sneaky Pete. Long sleeves and collars were Pete's choice mostly these days, so that the tapestry underneath was only hinted at. The long leg of a dark woman running out from under the sleeve, over the back of his hand. The vine growing up out of his chest, seeming to wind its way around a jugular vein. The dragon's tail that tickled his right earlobe.

By the time Pete and Joanne caught up with him, Joanne sounding like a castanet band as she swayed with her trinkets, Davey was staring intently at his own forearm while the tattooist colored a falcon there. When the coloring was done, Davey scanned the rows and rows of stencils lining the six-foot pegboards all around. The tattooist, with a face that dared anyone to smile, looked blankly at Davey.

"Another one," Davey said. The man put out his hand, to be paid.

"Give him another one," Pete snapped.

"You payin'?"

"I'm payin'."

"What do you want, kid?" the man asked as Pete paid him the first five dollars.

Davey looked over the ships, women, birds, big cats, Warner Brothers cartoons—Yosemite Sam with guns blazing, Roadrunner, Tasmanian Devil—but couldn't land on one. "What are those?" he said when he saw a pile of stencils on the floor.

"That's just shit, kid. Trash. Ruined by carnival idiots spilling Coke, puttin' their shitty cotton candy hands all over it, stompin 'em in the mud."

Davey gave the man the big-eye stare.

"Go look for yourself, then. It's just a waste."

Davey walked around behind the tattooist and picked the pile off the ground. He leafed through fifteen or so stencils, mostly the same stuff, plus a soggy dragon and a Christ head with the waffle of a hiking boot stomped into it. Then he stopped leafing, considered the image in his hand. It was a small one, a cowboy on a horse at full gallop, an old Remington image, but the top of the picture, from the chin up to almost the top of the ten-gallon hat, was burned away by a cigarette or cigar ash.

"I want this." Davey said, shoving the cowboy in the man's hand and sitting himself back in the chair.

"But this is garbage, kid."

Davey stuck out his hand, pointed to the back of it. "I want it right there. Then I want you to do the same thing on the other hand."

The tattooist looked up to Pete, who said, "You heard him. Do it."

So Davey got the faceless cowboy on both hands, and did not stop looking at them. "Pretty stupid, Davey," Joanne said. Davey just kept on walking, head down, as they headed out of the carnival. As they neared the gate an old veteran belly dancer, with a lot of extra belly hanging over her gauzy harem pants, shimmied to direct people into the fun-house freak museum. She reached out and lifted Davey's chin off his chest with two long purple nails. Davey stopped, startled for a second, and leaned back away. Until she smiled, swiveled, and stroked his cheek with the back of her hand.

Davey then reached his hand out, with Joanne behind him snapping, "Cut that out," and laid his hand flat on the dancer's soft middle. Looking at it. Looking at his hand on it.

"You're disgusting," Joanne said, walking on. Sneaky Pete clapped his boy on the shoulder and ushered him out.

On the way back, the three of them pressed together on the bench seat of Pete's El Camino, Pete said. "You guys gotta get right home?"

"Ya, right." Joanne sniffed. Davey shrugged.

"Wanna see my place?"

"Sure," said Joanne, who was increasingly happy to go to anybody's place rather than her own.

"Okay," Davey said, holding his hands in prayer position, then quickly flipping them over and back to make a sort of moving picture out of his cowboys.

Pete brought them to his motel, which was next door to a sub shop that looked like the tower of Pisa. A one-story, L-shaped building, the motel was white with white shutters and a white cement walk leading to each door. Inside Pete's room was almost nothing. A double bed, a night table, an oil painting of a waterfall in the middle of a forest, with a lot of mist and pine trees edged with snow of titanium white.

"No phone, no food, no pets, lots and lots of cigarettes," Pete said. "King of the road." He plunked himself down on the bed, pulled a tall green warm bottle of Haffenreffer malt liquor out of the nightstand drawer, and got right to the point.

"You kids want to come to Florida? You can, y'know. Say the word and the three of us'll hop in El Cam right this minute and be in Fort Lauderdale by the weekend. I sure would love to have you kids. We could even visit Gary. Jesus, Gary would be thrilled."

Joanne and Davey stood just inside the doorway. Davey stopped looking at his tattoos, looked briefly at Sneaky Pete, then at Joanne.

"Wow," Joanne said, a big grin peeling across her face. She sat on the edge of the bed. "Let's go."

Pete took a long drink, slammed the bottle down, then clapped one loud clap. "Alll riiight," he said, turning to Davey.

Davey took a step back, groped behind him for the door-knob without looking, opened the door. "Ah, um, thanks, Dad. For, y'know, everything. I gotta go now. Mum'll be missing me by now, so . . . I gotta go."

He disappeared out the door and started walking the quarter mile toward home. Pete sat speechless. Joanne stared at the door, then slowly turned back to Sneaky Pete.

"You know, right. That I can't leave him. I can't," Joanne said sadly.

She stood up. Pete stood up next to her and nodded. They went out together, caught up to Davey, and all walked home in the chill beginning of the night.

MUTHUH

"Where have you two been?" Lois said in that fuzzy low growl that held more violence than any scream.

"Where the *act*ion is," Joanne mocked.

Lois was rushing toward Joanne, open hand raised, when Pete stepped through the door. "And what the hell do you think *you're* doin'?" Pete yelled.

Lois jumped back, her hand covering her thrumming heart. She had no idea Sneaky Pete, or anyone else, was there.

"Oh," she said, recovering in a shot. "I would have known it was you. Who the hell do you think—"

"Lois, if I catch you hitting these kids, you can just kiss 'em good-bye, 'cause I'll take 'em to Florida. I'll take 'em legally, and I'll take 'em so far deep into the 'Glades the 'gators'll eat ya before you can find 'em. And if they don't eat ya, *I'll* kick your ass."

"You want to talk about legal, Pete? *You* don't want to talk about legal do you?"

"What is your problem, anyway, Lois? Afraid the kids are enjoying themselves?"

"Ya, great entertainment, Pete. Look at them." She gestured toward the living room, where Davey had slunk to the couch and was tapping the crystal on one of his two-dollar watches to get it working. Then she pointed at Joanne, who still stood next to her father and who, on cue, shook her wrists limply to make them clank and tinkle with cheese jewelry.

"They look like *you* for god's sake, you sleazy bastard!" Lois hollered.

"Speakin' of sleazy, where were you anyway when I came and took 'em, huh, Lois?"

"Get out of here, Peter. Just get your deadbeat ass out of my house. And the next time you break in here, I'm calling the police."

"Next time I break in, you probably won't be here then either."

"Out," Lois said, pointing at the door.

Sneaky Pete walked right up to Lois, who continued to point, then walked past her. He went to Davey on the couch.

Davey had the TV on now, and loud, but he wasn't looking at it. He was looking at his tattoos.

"Thanks for a sweet time, Davey," Pete said. "You guys really make it for me, y'know." Davey looked up into Pete's face, and Pete stooped to kiss him on his great expanse of forehead. "Whenever you need me, you call, okay?"

"Okay, Dad," Davey said, then looked away from Pete, at the tattoos again, then at the TV.

Pete passed again by Lois, who remained like a pointing mannequin. When he reached Joanne, she hugged him around the waist and rubbed her face back and forth over his chest.

"You sure?" he said.

"No, I'm not," she answered. "But I can't."

"Okay, sweetheart," Pete said. "I'll see you soon."

"Oh no you won't," Lois snapped.

"Oh yes he *will*," Joanne spat.

Sneaky Pete smiled at Lois as he backed out the door. "Lo, I gotta tell ya, you're one sucky muthuh."

He just managed to pull the door closed as Lois ricocheted a shoe off it, screaming without words.

"Take better care of 'em, Lois," Pete called on his way down the stairs, "or I'll know . . ."

Standing there with one shoe on, Lois stared at the door, fought back tears before speaking to Joanne. "What did he mean, Joanne, 'Are you sure'?"

"None of your business." Joanne fully expected a smack when she said it, but she didn't care.

Lois didn't move. She asked again, more quietly, "What was he talking about?"

"What are you, *jealous*? Because he likes me and he doesn't like you?" Like a shark Joanne could taste this kind of thing when it was happening, and she bit. She felt herself getting stronger, more pugnacious, while Lois faded. "Because you're just an old *rag* and *I'm not*? Huh, Ma?" With the words, Joanne marched right up to her mother and stood there, arms at her sides, practically demanding to be hit. Even Davey looked in from the other room, briefly, before turning away again.

But Lois didn't move. She continued to stare at the door, over Joanne's head, but now let the tears roll.

"The only thing I can do for you now is to tell you this, Jo. Don't hold on so tight to being a young thing. Because while you may remain pretty and you may remain smart and you may get rich, the one thing in this world you can be absolutely sure about is that one day, maybe soon, you will not be young anymore. And everybody's going to know it, and nothing else is going to matter."

Joanne stood, quiet, waiting. "Ya, so?"

When Lois didn't answer, Joanne just walked around her and went to her room.

"Ya, so . . . ," Lois repeated.

When Joanne came out an hour later expecting to find her supper, she found instead Lois hugging Davey with both arms while he sat staring blankly at the TV. He wore her as calmly as if she were a parrot sitting on his shoulder. Joanne made macaroni and cheese for all of them and they ate in dead silence.

Lois was out of bed at dawn the next morning, reading out of an old yellow Betty Crocker cookbook as she tried to make real pancakes. Puffs of flour dust rose gently, then faded to the table or the floor as she first picked out the tiny brown mealybugs then poured carefully into the measuring cup. An eggshell fragment the size of a fingernail trimming was going to have to stay in the mix after Lois buried it deeper by chasing after it. With every flick of the whisk more batter spilled over the side of the bowl, but it *was* batter. She tasted it with her finger. She was good at this, some time ago, and the taste of the wet batter reminded her of that.

She pulled a half box of breakfast sausages from the freezer. She didn't remember buying them. The box was wide open and the links were crusted in a quarter inch of spiny white frost. That wouldn't matter, though, after the boiling. Lois always boiled sausages before browning them, to reduce the fat.

Lois had just nodded off at the table when the children

crept stiffly into the kitchen. They didn't sit down at first, stood there mesmerized at the mess of cooking stuff all over, and at the actual early-morning presence of their mother. Joanne raised her nose in the air and whiffed the sausages that were warming in the oven. Davey stuck his finger in the dripping bowl that sat on the table, tasted it, then pulled back like he'd seen something wiggling in there.

Lois's eyes opened slowly, followed a few seconds later by full awareness. She was embarrassed. "Come on, sit down," she said, jumping up and making herself busy. She slapped plates and silverware down, dropped one dollop, then four into the sizzling skillet, and in a few minutes served pancakes, sausages, and sectioned fresh oranges to her gape-mouthed baby birds. Joanne and Davey ate quickly, ravenously, not out of a great hunger, exactly, but out of a *desire* for this food right here. Between bites they would tip glances up at Lois, who was smiling as she watched, smiling satisfied, but smiling tired.

The meal finished, the kids sat back pregnant with round bellies and with feelings they didn't know, things they couldn't get out. Lois disappeared briefly into the bathroom and returned with a comb to attack the mop that was always on Davey's head. The comb got impossibly stuck an inch above his forehead, and she pulled it out with a laugh. Joanne gave her mother a weak smile and tapped Davey on the shoulder, and they got up. "Thanks, Mum," Davey said as Jo led him out to school. "Thanks, Mum."

"You want me to take care of that, Davey?" Joanne said hurriedly, pointing at his tattoo. "I'm sure I could take that right out in no time. With cold cream."

"No thanks," he said, walking away with his hands clasped behind his back. He'd already touched up both tattoos to keep them alive a little longer, working with either hand, with a pen.

When they were gone, Lois looked around at the kind of domestic mess she hadn't witnessed in years. Dirty dishes, heavy batter solidifying on the table, the floor, the stove. Every container she'd opened sitting open. Eggshells and orange peels sitting in the sink. The entire room seeming to be powdered in flour.

She stood up to work on it. The smile left her, the flutter of joy in her belly gone with it. The tiredness returned in its place. Lifelessly she picked up the batter bowl and trucked it toward the sink. The bowl slipped out of her buttery hand and exploded like a smashed windshield on the floor. Lois stared down at it, stood on it, and quietly began to cry again. She couldn't do this. Not really, not for real, not for long, not even for one more meal, she already knew. She couldn't do this. She couldn't do *this*.

Joanne came back through the kitchen door, making

Davey wait outside for her. She *could* do it, she thought after she'd left. She could tell her mother thank you. But Joanne was stunned all over again to find the abandoned kitchen, the untouched mess, to crush under her feet the smashed pieces of glass. She walked to her mother's bedroom and found her lying under the blankets, coiled on her side, staring at her music box, which was open and tinkling "Nadia's Theme." As it would play for Lois all day long.

Joanne crept back out of the room. She cleaned the kitchen so thoroughly it was hard to remember the breakfast scene. Then she went out and collected Davey, who still waited, forty minutes and late for school, on the step.

THEY

They want to take Jo's baby away. I don't know who they are but they are making a mistake because they can't have him. Because I don't care I really don't what they say or what they think or whatever about how maybe Jo does or can or doesn't or can't take care of the baby Dennis but it's all just stupid as hell because I can take care of the baby Dennis and that's that.

They said that maybe 'cause Jo isn't there at the house all the time and because her old man like she calls him isn't there at all and because the baby Dennis spent too much time with nobody stopping him from standing up in his little cracked painted crib that was mine a long time ago that Ma said Jo stole but if it was mine I say he can have it so never mind Ma and Jo and all their stuff. Staring out the window chewing enough of the paint off the side of the crib and some more off the windowsills when he goes there to stare some more that now he has to go to children's hospital every week and let them look at his blood and he has to take some medicine they think that's the reason that maybe he should get taken away.

But who doesn't stare out the window is what I say. If I had a nickel for every hour I spent staring out the window at maybe a cloud that looks like my mother's ice-white pretty face or at the rain that looks like the drops grow and grow into blobby clear water balloons as they get closer to the ground because I have eyes good enough that I can zero in on one single one from all that far away. Or at a star in the purple at night. For a million hours I could do that. Well if I had a nickel for all the times I did that I'd just have a lot of money is what I'd have.

And *I* make him take his medicine anyway. All the time just like he's supposed to I make him swallow it even though he hates it and he gets crazy and he hates me for giving it to him and he slaps me and scratches me and kicks me and there is nothing nothing that can hurt me like my baby Dennis trying to hurt me. I used to come just some days but now I come practically every day because Jo isn't so serious as maybe she ought to be about giving the baby Dennis his medicine and once she found out that I was very serious about it I think that just maybe she forgot a couple of times on purpose just to make sure I'd come and boom she could get out of the apartment like on a rocket ship. And giving me two glasses of wine now because she's so happy to be going and I'm so happy to be staying.

But some of the things she does like they say because the law makes her like she does take him to children's hospital all the time. I tell her maybe I should go with her sometimes so that I can understand things more and so she doesn't maybe forget or not care enough about something the doctor might be telling her to do. She tells me to forget it and that once the doctors get a load of me they'll take the baby Dennis and they'll take me and they'll throw her Joanne into jail for conducting experiments at home so I should shut up and drink my grape and leave the fucking mothering to her is the end of what she tells me.

And when they told her she had to move out of that old house because it wasn't safe for the baby Dennis she did but she moved to another house that had the same unsafe stuff in it because she found out about this thing where you don't have to pay any rent if the landlord doesn't take care of the problems so she does that not paying rent for a few months until she gets chased out and can find another unsafe place. So you keep the goddamn baby away from the goddamn windowsills Davey is what she says about it and is that so hard that it shouldn't be a decent trade all that rent money that can go to food that will fill the baby up and he won't want to be eating no windowsills like he does. Only I haven't seen hundreds of bucks of new food going into the baby Dennis since all this started.

But all the bad stuff was when I wasn't here when I didn't know but now I am and now I do so they can stay away now they can leave us alone now. But I know they won't. But they don't know me though. What I would do. What I would do if I ever knew that they were coming here to get my baby Dennis I would take him and put him on my bike the one that my dad left for me in my room at night the bike that is tougher and faster than anything and that nobody or no thing can touch me when I'm on it. I'd take my baby Dennis and I'd put him in the front of a milk crate wrapped in a heavy blanket just like Eliot and E.T. in the movie we'd touch our fingers together they would glow and I'd pedal hard and he would make the bike fly so we couldn't be caught and I know Joanne would let me do it.

We'd be up there away from everybody my heart would glow right through my skin right through my shirt and the baby Dennis's would too because we're just like in *E.T.* the same he's just like me and I'm just like him all connected up he feels everything I feel I feel everything he feels he feels everything I feel.

And I'd ride him all the way up to the star that both of us are always looking at out the window is what I would do.

GIMP

When the orders eventually changed from "Joanne, dammit, you stay in this house and take care of your brother" to "Joanne, dammit, would you get that Davey up and out of the house for a change," Joanne was out the door like a heat-seeking missile, with Davey in tow.

She introduced him to her friends, who actually didn't do much more with their time than Davey did, but they did it outside and in a large group. They spent their weekends and afternoons hanging out draped all over one another, boys and girls mostly ages twelve to fifteen, just like a pride of heat-prostrated lions, on the porch of a family whose parents seemed to be nonexistent and whose daughter Celeste was more or less the group's leader. Joanne was scared, bringing her little brother to this place, but he was hers, and they were hers, so she was going to do it.

The problem was whenever somebody brought along a new hanger, the first order of business was typically to give him a beating before letting him stay. But that wouldn't be a problem this time. Davey was just a kid, too young for that kind of stuff. And he was so sweet and no trouble to nobody. He was Davey. Anyway, not while Joanne was around. No way.

Big old Celeste, who some of the kids called "Brutus" when she wasn't in earshot, came right toward Davey the first time Joanne brought him around. "Yo, Jo, who's the gimp?" she said, getting it started.

There was nothing wrong with Davey, not really. Nothing physical. Nothing outside of a few too many hours spent alone. Lately in front of a TV of course, or on his bike riding furiously to nowhere, talking to no one, stopping for nothing, until he'd gone out ten, fifteen, twenty miles and only the fading light told him it was time to come back. The glaze came from not talking enough to other human beings. The prominent forehead and the height—Davey was, at nine, already five feet six inches—came from his father, Sneaky Pete. The crooked Prince-Valiant-meets-Julius-Caesar haircut that exaggerated it all was courtesy of Lois. "Goddammit, Davey, you look like a sheepdog, staring out of that bang-work, and you haven't got the brains to even brush it out of your way." So, one big snip. The overall look was a mistake, was all, too much head, too much height, too much quiet, too much dumb sweet. Just an unfair, unfortunate mistake.

"He's my brother," Joanne said coolly. "And he ain't no gimp."

"You never said nothin' about havin' no half-wit at home." Celeste laughed, making others laugh too.

But Joanne knew how quickly, in a circle like hers, the casual remark became the permanent identity, so she did what she had to do. She walked right up and smacked her in the mouth.

"Go, Jo, go, Jo," a handful of the kids yelled as they jumped to their feet to watch the two girls tumble down the stairs.

"Kill her, Celeste," somebody yelled. "Snatch her bald. Rip her face off."

They were all twined up, the two girls looking like a single alligator caught in a net and twisting, rolling, slapping on the ground. Joanne had Celeste's long loose black hair wrapped around and around her fist like a cowboy roping a bronco. Celeste, from her position on her back, had both arms outstretched, both hands on Joanne's face, both sets of long nails digging into the face. Celeste dug in and pulled at the flesh, her thumbnails catching inside Joanne's mouth and pulling the lip up to make her look like a snarling dog. Joanne started listing one way, looking about to tumble over, as Celeste's fingernails caught the lower rim of both eyes and started ripping down.

Davey watched, like everybody else. Inside, in his stomach and in his chest and in his temples, he was sick. He was screaming. He was wielding an aluminum baseball bat, raising it high over his head, and bringing it crashing down on Celeste's head. He could see it like it was happening, Celeste falling with no life in her rolled-back eyes, falling with her face right on Davey's shoes, the soak of blood warming his toes. And the disgusting animals beside him, across from him, behind him, in the fight-circle that had formed on the sidewalk, all backing away giving Davey his due as he helped his wounded sister off the ground. Inside, it all happened. Outside, he did nothing but look on, hyperventilate so shallowly that you had to put an ear to his lips to tell, and wipe his eye once.

As she was about to fall, to land on *her* back with Celeste on top—the certain death spot—Joanne pumped her fist one hard time. The fist with the hair in it. Everyone heard it, the scrape and bang sound like a baseball landing in a parking lot. Celeste stopped clawing momentarily, stunned. So Joanne did it again, *BANG*. Celeste just tried to push Joanne away now, or hold her off, rather than attack, but it was no use. Joanne finally got her other hand close enough to grab more hair and, with two good grips, pounded and pounded and pounded Celeste's head on the pavement. People stopped cheering. Blood started showing, a spot, a blot, a puddle, on the sidewalk behind Celeste's head as well as on her face, dripping from Joanne's mouth. Out of the crowd, one boy grabbed Joanne's left arm, one her right.

And it was over just like that. Joanne got up peacefully, as if a timer had sounded or a referee had declared it over. Gradually the whole pride went back to flopping in their spots. Two girls and a boy helped Celeste up and took her, crying lowly and spitting, into the house. Joanne pulled Davey by the hand and sat on the bottom step. Shaking, but silent, looking everybody in the eye.

The blood, a red cloud floating on the white concrete, was the only sign that anything had happened.

There was a slap on Joanne's shoulder, then another, and she started feeling a little good. Nobody said anything about it, but she knew what she'd done. Celeste, hated though she was, was still the queen, but she was more of a figurehead now. Joanne had the *real stuff*. Then she felt Davey's hand lightly touching her face. He reached out and laid two fingers on the hurt part just below one eye, ran the fingers down slowly over the long skid marks of nail that ran straight to her mouth where the gums were still bleeding. She grabbed his hand there, put it back in his own lap, turned away, and spat some blood.

She looked at him. But what had she done for *him*? This is what she knew. She knew, before she'd even put a hand on Celeste, that there was nothing she could really do about the gimp thing or the half-wit thing or any other thing anybody wanted to pull on Davey. But what she *had* done, the one and only thing she always knew she *could* do for him, was that she made sure it wouldn't happen while *she* was around. She had that one nugget of the universe to hold, and she'd held it. It wasn't much, but it was the one thing she could truly, surely do for him.

Joanne's hulking, mumbling, grimy sometimes boyfriend Phil came over and wedged his big butt between Davey and Joanne on the step. "Pretty tough, babe," he said, kissing her on the bloody lip, then licking it off. "But, ah, but you know, you know how it is here, don'tcha?"

She straightened up, fear finally in her face.

"Well, what, Jo?" he said, as if the situation were honestly out of his hands. "Did you think you could go around it? Jus' 'cause you say no?"

"No, Phil," she pleaded, grabbing his hand. "He's only little."

"Ain't neither, babe. He's big as you. Not too much behind me, even."

"But, Phil, he's only—"

Phil held up his great big hand, walling her off. "But I tell you what we can do. Because it's you, Joanne. Maybe we can make a sorta axception."

Joanne relaxed.

"Hold on a second," Phil said, turning away from Joanne toward Davey. Davey looked up at Phil, the wide eyes waiting, like always.

With a quick flick of his forearm, Phil punched Davey. Cracked him in the eye a half-speed poke about like a Ping-Pong stroke. He didn't follow through, pulled his meaty fist back as soon as it landed. His concession to Davey and Joanne.

Everyone sat frozen, even Joanne. Phil stood up over Davey, who had fallen backward and now lay over two steps, holding his eye.

"And that's it." Phil addressed the crowd, who didn't seem to care. "This young man is all paid up." He leaned over and pulled Davey up to sitting position, "What is your name again?"

"Davey," Davey answered, removing his hand to expose an already swelling, bluing eye.

"Nobody hits Davey no more."

"Yo Phil, yo Phil, yo Phil," the lions chanted, something they'd clearly had to practice for.

Phil sat back down next to Joanne. "See, babe, I took care a ya."

Joanne looked at nobody. Tears welled in her eyes but did not fall. Instead she tipped her head back and spit. Spit blood, through the space in her front teeth, a high, arcing stream better than any ballplayer with tobacco juice, clearing the sidewalk to land in the oily street.

Davey leaned toward Joanne, right over Phil as if he weren't there. "You okay, Jo?" he asked. "You need me?"

She just leaned back on her elbows and stared off blankly, like the rest of the lions. Phil put his arm around her and leered. Jo sighed but didn't resist. Now Phil had to be repaid. For his kindness.

REGULAR COOL

I'm on my bike. It's cool on my bike. Always is, cool, the *only* place that is. I don't mean cool like aren't I the big man and doesn't everybody wish he was me. I just mean regular cool. Like the weather isn't so hot on my bike the way it seems to be everywhere else. The breeze puffs nice over my brow and stops the heat that's always under there. And I've got a *lot* of brow.

And with the cooling, the thoughts, my thoughts, come easy and orderly and slow the way I figure everybody else's thoughts come all the time.

I stayed on my bike one time, last weekend, for twenty-four hours straight. Mostly just to see if I could do it. Not moving every second of the time, but pretty much. Sometimes I took a break to just straddle the bike for a few minutes and watch stuff, but then I'd get all nervous and sweaty and jumbled again until I pedaled it away. Where I went in twenty-four hours of biking was everywhere. I rode out ten miles late Saturday afternoon, all the way to the quarry. Sometimes I can go to the quarry and find nobody there and I can scream, loud enough and long enough so that I nearly pass out, and then I can stand there and listen to myself scream back at me. But on a Saturday afternoon you don't find nobody at the quarry, you find a bunch of kids drinking beer in tall cans and pony bottles, smashing the bottles on rocks right near me with a pop like dropping a lightbulb. Kids with air rifles who shoot frogs in the water and who see a kid like me and start to run in my direction and say things like "Hmmm humm, maybe we ought to get the pants off of this young man and see what we got." So I didn't stay but a couple of minutes at the quarry before I pedaled so hard my great mountain bike that I got from my dad that I kicked up rocks and a cloud of quarry dust big as a hot air balloon.

I rode the ten miles back into town, which is where I spent the rest of the time. Riding, looking at everybody. Riding up close to the little kids at the park because I cannot get enough of little kids at parks. I could go on watching that, little kids playing on the swings and slides and turtles mounted on great big springs that coil up out of the ground, I could watch it forever even if I wasn't on my bike. I smile there like no place else in the world just because I can't help it. I can feel the difference in my face, the muscles all stretched out and tired at the corners of my mouth and on the balls of my cheekbones. And they like me back, little kids, because they run up to me and slap the fence with sticks and poke their tongues out at me and smile just as big as I do. But every time, I feel it, and I have to go. The deep heat of the stares I'm getting from the mothers who are sitting on the benches and sipping diet tonics and talking to each other but looking at me. And they're all now scowling, or frightened, and then one or two or four of them stand up and inch their way my way and I have to go before they reach me.

But I think I saw just about everything in town last weekend. That'll happen when you ride for twenty-four hours. A lot of those hours though, the latest ones and the earliest ones especially, there's not much to see except in the places Ma tells me not to go. "There." Don't go "there," she tells me. Stay out of "there." But I realized a while ago that there was about half the world I'd never see if I didn't pass through "there" sometimes, so I started doing it.

Turned out she was wrong about it anyway. Except for one time when they made a little circle around me, these guys with the sunglasses and baseball hats, and one of them said *"Maybe*, you're gonna hafta give up the cycle, junior." Well I just sat there on the bike and I looked at him and I didn't say a thing. I slowly crouched down low over the handlebars, practically lying on the bike the way a jockey does with his horse, and I wrapped my arms around it. I kept looking up at the man. Because he couldn't have it, whether he was one big scary man—which he was—or six big scary men with their arms folded across their chests—which they were. They could not have the bike. It was then just as it is now and will be tomorrow, that you can take my bike if you have to take it but you're going to have to take my life along with it. Because that's what you'd be doing anyway, taking my life when you took my bike.

So I got to keep it, I guess because I made everybody laugh so much the way I hugged onto my bike like I was going to keep it from them. "Go on now, goofy kid," the man said to me. His name was Lester, and I did go on when he told me to.

But I went back. I passed through there all the time, sometimes day and sometimes night, because I was forever riding and there are just not enough places in this world to ride if you ride forever. Unless you ride out and don't come back. "Whatcha doin' back here, little crazy boy," Lester said when he saw me again. I rode in a circle around him, around and around the way I would when I wanted to see something up close but I didn't want to stop riding. The circle got tighter and tighter until I could keep my balance while buzzing in a four-foot circle like a circus trick rider. Lester liked that, standing in the center with his arms folded trying to follow me from behind his sunglasses without moving his head.

"Riding," I answered. "I like to ride."

"I guess you do," he said, and we began having little conversations like that all the time. Sometimes I would ride that way just to have the thirty-second talk with Lester.

"You back *again*? Boy, don't you got no home?"

"I got one." I circled and circled him.

"Then go there," he snapped, stamping his foot. I took off, whizzing down the street, but it was play. Lester was the person who never really chased me off.

"Gypsy boy," Lester said next time. I could tell he was starting to like seeing me. If I didn't come by one day, he'd be twice as excited the next. "The boy with no home. The day-and-night cycler."

"You're always here, too," I said. "You got no home?"

Lester smiled, nodding. He was like a flashing neon light as I spun around him. His big electric smile with the two gold front teeth on one side, the six-inch gold lettering L-E-S-T-E-R flashing across his black satin baseball jacket in back.

"What is your name, boy?" Lester asked.

"Davey," I said as I peeled away, suddenly feeling the need to fly.

"Gypsy Davey," he called after me. "There go the Gypsy Davey."

So when Lester and his friends saw me time after time after time during my twenty-four hours, he didn't think anything of it other than to say, after a while, "Gypsy boy, y'know, if you're gonna do all this motoring around for nothin', then here, why don't you take this little package over to so-and-so street and give it to so-and-so little man and here, keep this little fi' dollars for your trouble."

And I did it. Lester was pretty happy when I came back, and he gave me another package and another five dollars. And then one more. But I asked him, after the last time, when the person I brought the package to came out to the sidewalk in some leopard-skin bikini underwear, with a gun in his hand and a baby on his hip, I asked Lester if he'd be mad if I didn't go to any more houses. Lester didn't mind, and I hung around some more until my twenty-four was up and I went home Sunday afternoon to sleep for about twenty-four more. On my way in the house Ma said, "You missed lunch, Davey."

But now I'm back. I'm rested and I'm on my bike and I'm at the quarry. But it's not Saturday afternoon and the place is all mine. I passed the playground and drew a stare, even though I didn't even slow down. I wish I could tell them. I wish they could see how I take care of the baby Dennis, so then they could feel better and I could feel better. But I can't and they can't because there just seem to be things that can't work that way.

I scream across the quarry, like I'm blowing all my air out, and the scream and the air sails out and over, bounces off the far granite, then comes back to me like I wanted it to.

BIG NOW

Joanne was tired. A very tired fifteen. Where she used to flop with her friends, just like her friends, leaning back on her elbows on the steps killer cool like she wasn't lazy, just too mean and pubescent pretty to care, now she lay flat out, wasted. Stretching herself across the middle step of Celeste's porch, she didn't care about people stepping over her, didn't care about sunburn, didn't care if somebody, maybe Phil or maybe somebody else, got an urge to reach out and grab a quick piece of feel now and then. Long as they didn't squeeze too hard or too long.

Davey minded, but he learned to live with it. Learning to live with it. That was what he seemed to be learning best. Lois taught him, the way she taught everything, by accident. Joanne taught him. And Joanne's friends—who she once called "The Lions," but now dismissed as "The Dogs," even as she failed to quit them—taught him. Phil, alpha male, king of the lions, lead dog, Joanne's *thing*, bigger than the rest, so that was how everything was decided, Phil was an educator.

So if big old Phil was smoking a little dope one day and feeling a little generous and decided to blow dumb old skinny Gypsy Davey a little shotgun just for a hoot and to relax the boy, then who was there to say that wasn't okay? Because even though he sat still as a floorboard and hardly said a croak, he gave off a tenseness that made Phil squirm.

"There you go, sonny," Phil said from behind a glassy-eyed grin. "Now recline, and stop bein' so tight all the time."

So who was there to say that it wasn't okay?

Not Davey, who breathed the smoke in deep, held it as long as he could like he'd seen everyone else do, then coughed a wheezy, painful cough for five minutes.

Not Joanne, who lifted her head off the step for a few seconds, looked at the hunched and heaving back of her little brother with some concern, then let her heavy head drop again. She slapped his back weakly from her repose.

So who was there to say it wasn't okay?

So what if Davey's head started snapping at every movement on the street, every passing car, every skinny cat, every wad of spit that flew over from the crowd behind him, like he was watching a tennis match at five thousand RPMs. And so what if he was starting to list to one side a little? Who wasn't, right? Joanne reached out and straightened him up and gave his back a reassuring rub to calm him until the next help-less tilt when she did it again. He turned his great cow eyes to her, lost, begging—still without speaking—for her to right not just his posture, but the world around his head.

"Stop that," she said, "stop looking at me, Davey." She pushed his face away, turning it back out toward the street. It was the kind of thing that at first gave her a shudder, a scared-little-girl crackling of the heart, to watch what she watched happen to Davey. But it was the kind of thing she would get used to fairly quickly at this point, if he only wouldn't look at her too much. She felt, like she felt for herself, that this all would be better for the kid anyway. She was too tired to feel it any other way. She took a toke, and she felt it more.

So who was there to say that it wasn't okay?

Walking home, Joanne played a hunch that wasn't exactly a guess. "You hungry, Davey?"

He panted, as if he'd been holding his breath and could now let go. "Oh Jo, I'm so hungry I'm gonna eat my clothes if I don't get something."

She laughed at him loud enough to make him smile. "Then why didn't you say something?"

"I didn't know. Didn't know if I was *supposed* to be hun-gry, or not. I was afraid of sounding like a dip."

Still laughing and shaking her head, Joanne roughly grabbed him by the collar and manhandled him through the glass doors of DoDo's Roast Beef. She loved roughing him up because he'd gotten so tall that she had to stand on tiptoe to do it. And because Davey let her do it.

DoDo's stayed open every night till three a.m., and that was when they did most of their business. At that time of night, their pizza rolls, onion rings, and gristly red meat swimming in sauce were like milk and cookies to the kind of people who were out scaring up food. Those were the same people who were there in the daytime too, only fewer because most were still sleeping.

Joanne fished through her jacket pockets, the breast pockets, inside wallet pockets, outside hand pockets. She wedged her hands into her packed-tight-to-the-skin jeans pockets, front and back, until she'd squeezed out every dime she had. Then she shook down Davey, jostling, spinning, groping, and frisking him clean. The haul was $3.80, enough for a small Beefy with cheese and a pizza roll.

They sat in a booth, where Joanne divided the items almost evenly with a white plastic knife. Davey had already swallowed his half of the pizza roll before she'd managed to saw through the beef. In two minutes, their places, with untouched napkins lying square and white in front of them, looked so clean it appeared they were *awaiting* their food rather than done.

"I'm gonna eat this napkin, Jo," Davey said in total seri-ousness. "I'm hungrier now than before we ate."

"Me too," she said.

They got up to go, but just before they reached the door, Joanne noticed a couple, middle-agey and shadowy in the corner booth. The kind of people Joanne always found to be easy marks when she wanted to hit strangers up for money, which she liked to do when she was stoned, whether she had money on her or not. People always paid her to go away quickly when they were eating.

"'Scuse me folks, but me and my simpleton brother were trying to get us something to eat. No shit, he's got them gen-uine I'm-a-idiot cards, but he's havin' a new batch printed right now—"

Joanne could see the man, a small, rotund, blue-faced creature with active sweat, was immediately ready to crumble to her. But it was Jo who buckled first when the woman who had been hanging under the floppy hat and cigarette smoke looked up, and was Lois.

It was almost difficult to recognize Lois still—even as she pushed her face menacingly toward Joanne—under the heavy poundage of eye makeup she was sporting. Yet Lois it was, her mother, though she was not about to admit it.

"Get away," Lois snapped. Her date said nothing.

When she realized the tack her mother was taking,

Joanne regained power. Davey, paranoid, terribly confused, stepped behind Joanne.

"Please, lady," Joanne moaned. "We're destitute. We eat garbage. We live in the street. Our mother is a—"

"Get . . . away," Lois growled with such crackling low menace that the bald man and Joanne both pulled back from her. But Jo would not quit.

"We should just give them something," the man said timidly. "They do look pretty bad off. Look at their eyes."

Davey now hid his face completely, but Joanne turned her own dewy, reddened cow eyes on Lois and the man.

"Leo . . . ," Lois warned.

"Here you are," Leo said, pressing a ten-dollar bill into Jo's hand.

"Bless you, bless you," Joanne said, bowing as she backed away, into Davey. "And thank you too, Mom, I mean ma'am." Davey started pulling Joanne backward by the jacket, toward the exit.

"Hell no," she said. "We're eatin'."

Jo took the money up to the counter and piled it on. Two more pizza rolls, two more sandwiches—*big* Beefys this time—onion rings and large Cokes.

"To go?" Davey said hopefully over her shoulder.

"No go," she said, and led him back toward the booths, past the near booths, down the aisle, to the far corner again.

They sat down in the booth directly across from Lois and Leo's.

Joanne smiled sweetly at the couple when they looked at her, then popped an onion ring in her mouth. Davey shrank down in the seat, but still ate, and started giving the fish eye to his mother's other man.

"Maybe we should go now," Lois said.

"In a minute," Leo said, sipping coffee out of a tall yellow paper cup.

Lois tried to ignore, but couldn't keep her eyes off the scene in the next booth. Jo was spinning onion rings like greasy little hula hoops around her fingers before eating them. She was taking bites out of her sandwich so big that she couldn't close her mouth fully to chew them. In the middle of it all she was seized by a giggling fit that would not stop, making her gag on her food, cough little pieces across the table to land on her stunned brother's face. But the crowning event, the cherry on top, was when she very, slowly, very dramatically took a five-inch pizza roll and, turning to face her mother, pressed the whole thing gently into her own throat. Tilting her head back, like a sword-swallower, she lowered the entire roll down her gullet without so much as a catch. Just as it disappeared, along with thumb and index finger up to the knuckles, she slowly drew it all back out again, intact, dragging it out between her lips. Then she took just the daintiest bite out of the tip.

"Leo, we're going," Lois said, fairly leaping to her feet. Leo was slow to react, still sitting enraptured over the pizza-roll performance. Davey was the only one who missed it, having been occupied with staring daggers into Leo.

On his way by, Leo smiled and nodded at Jo, who winked in return. Lois simply pointed her finger at Jo like a gun, and showed all her teeth.

Jo seemed almost anxious to get home. Davey was terrified.

"Maybe we should go for a walk, huh, Jo?"

"What for? She's probably not home yet anyway. Y'know, gotta do a little somethin' for ol' Leo for buyin' the meal."

Davey put his hands over his ears, shook his head no ten, twenty, forty times, and started trotting ahead, away from Jo. Still covering his ears, still shaking his head.

Joanne caught up to him, ran in front of him, and made him stop. She faced him squarely and pulled his hands down from his ears. As he continued to shake his head no, she nodded her head yes. More, he shook. She nodded just as insistently.

"You gotta grow up, Davey. You gotta grow up."

He pulled away from her, she pulled him back with a yank.

"You *gotta . . . grow . . . up*. And you gotta do it right now. Davey, I been thinkin' about it and I don't think I can take care of you no more. I'm havin' a whole shitload of trouble takin' care of *me*, if you want to know the truth. You're big now, Davey, look at ya."

Davey did. He looked down at himself, mostly at the long legs that were growing up out the sidewalk like a pair of knobby blue jean beanstalks. Then he looked back at his sister. *Down* at her. Still, there was littleness in those big round sad eyes that Joanne couldn't look at anymore.

"Come on, Davey." She turned away and started walking quickly.

When they walked through the door, Lois stood straight ahead about eight feet away. Her feet were planted wide apart, and hanging from her left hand was a long three-inch-wide tooled leather belt with a fist-sized pewter skull buckle. A Sneaky Pete artifact.

"Do you know how hard I have to work to get a man to—"

"Uh-uh, no way," Joanne cut her off, pointing at the strap.

"Get out of here, Davey," Lois said in a gravelly voice. Davey stood petrified. Lois took a step toward Joanne. Then stopped abruptly when Joanne took a step toward *her*.

"We're through with that, shit, Lois," Joanne said, more of a warning, a final negotiation, than a threat.

"Oh, *Lois*, am I now? I don't know who you think you are these days, Joanne, but you better think again. Is it the drugs, perhaps, talking for you? Honey? Darling? Sweetheart?"

Those were the words. The words that were never heard in this house, spoken now with such furious, mocking insincerity. Joanne still cared, a little bit, about what her next action would be. Until those words.

"Davey, get the hell out of here." It was Joanne who said it this time. The result however, was the same; he stood.

Without warning Lois advanced, drew back the belt and snapped it like a cowboy. It cracked across Jo's leg, leaving a long red wasp sting on her thigh where the jeans were already ripped wide open. As Joanne coolly walked toward her mother, Lois lashed out the belt again, this time whipping her across the cheek.

Joanne stopped walking momentarily, covered her face with both hands. She made not a sound and resumed marching toward Lois. "Joanne, go to your room," Lois said in a final lame attempt to control Jo. As she spoke, she backpedaled, fear coming in a red wave over her face.

It had to happen. The time had come. If anyone had taught Joanne to be tough, even if she had done it accidentally, it was Lois. But Lois was getting weaker now, and Jo had become at fifteen a hard-assed, snaggletooth little sonofabitch. A lot tougher, really, than Lois ever was.

It was basically already over when Lois tried, half-heartedly, to raise the strap to her daughter one more time. Joanne's fist shot out like a baseball from a pitching machine, hitting her mother with a punch in the mouth at about ninety miles an hour, dropping her.

Joanne stood over Lois for a second as her mother writhed on the floor, covering up and crying. Then she reached down and picked up the belt.

Before she'd even straightened all the way up, Jo felt a grip on her wrist. Davey had finally moved. She didn't acknowledge him, continued looking down on her mother, until he jerked the belt out of her hand. Joanne stalked out of the house, paused in the doorway, slammed the door as hard as she could.

Davey picked his mother up off the floor and carried her to the couch.

US ALONE HAPPY

Gypsies always steal babies anyway right so it wouldn't be like no big surprise and they'll stop looking after only a little while I know because it'll just be like the big stupid one just run off with the little stupid one is what they all will say and then after everybody who's supposed to has done the right thing and made a nice show and sort of stood on all the porches whispering Davey oh Davey yoo-hoo are you out there and hello baby Dennis are you out there too then everybody can relax and stop pretending to look.

Then they can leave us alone happy. We'll be happy they'll be happy because nobody wants the baby Dennis but I do and nobody wants the maybe Davey but he does and so then I can be a hero for all of us am I right?

They'd probably want to give me some kind of medal is

what would probably happen if they wanted to tell the truth and if they could find me. Which they won't 'cause like I said they can't have him and like I said I would want to take him little baby Dennis to our star away like E.T. but I'm not stupid not a kid not a gimp I know I can't really do that but what I can be is somebody who could find a place that was just as far away and just as secret and just as quiet and not angry that the baby Dennis and me could go to. Better than a star even. I will get him there.

Gary says Florida is a place like that. Wrote me a letter from prison Gary did said I should get myself down there with him and Dad even though him and Dad aren't really together since Gary put that big hole in that little lady's head with the golf club. It could be the best he said 'cause these messed-up women won't be there to mess us up like they already done and Florida is a man's place and that as far as he was concerned our mother could just well do something to him that a guy shouldn't ought to say about his mother and while she's at it Joanne could just do it to him too.

I could go if it was such a good place for boys to go in Florida when they wanted to run off I could do it pedal all the way there with the baby Dennis in the milk crate on the handlebars and I would never get tired. That's what I would do if Florida was the right place for us except I won't be going there and sure won't be taking the baby Dennis there as long as Gary is there whether he's in a cell or not.

COME DANCING

Joanne was sixteen and a half and fat as a balloon when she married Gus the fruit truck driver. She said she loved him right away because he smelled delicious. The scent of bananas and melons and almost-turned peaches hung on him all the time, allowing her to somehow ignore Gus's droopy eyelids, the pants crotch that hung to his knees, and the stump of a ring finger on *each* hand that got ripped off in separate accidents with the heavy truck door and that probably said more about who Gus was than his aroma did.

But Gus was a hardworking man and, more importantly, a steady-working man. He had been driving that same fruit truck for Kassab Brothers' fruit market since he was Joanne's age, which was twelve years ago. That fact alone made him a good man, a good catch.

So even though it was obvious to the neighbors and the

altar boys and Gus's legally blind grandmother that Joanne was no more than a month away from motherhood, the wedding was greeted as an unqualified joyous event. All it took was a minor piece of alteration for Jo to fit into Lois's old white satin wedding gown, a proper bride, train trailing a block behind, since Lois of course was carrying a lot more than a second slice of carrot cake in her own belly when she wore it.

Sneaky Pete paid for the Sons of Italy hall. And for the church and the priest in a way. The local parish wouldn't do it, let the pregnant sixteen-year-old get married in the church, so Pete had to track down good old Father Waller who happened to owe Pete his life due to a little happening in a little room behind a little restaurant in the North End a few years back. Pete happened to be playing in a friendly card game in which the father—snazzy as hell in his Hawaiian shirt and huaraches, but a bit sweaty and red—made the mistake of playing too long after he had no money. Pete sponsored him to the people running the game, allowing Father Waller to keep his thumbs.

Which in the end meant Joanne and Gus could spend nine hours one Saturday before the wedding in *pre Cana,* answering questions about themselves and the sacraments and procreation. "Have you ever engaged in sexual activity?" the young priest asked, loosening his collar and looking away whenever he could.

"No sir," Joanne said proudly, happily, indestructibly, knowing her date in the church had been paid for and that her knight was, sleepily, at her side. "I'm just another local chubby chick made good."

Gus paid for the limousines. Limousines, more important than the church. More important than the white gown. More important than the tallest cake or the presence of all the favorite relatives or the Al Jolson Tan-o-Rama-skin-with-beige-lipstick wedding announcement picture on the back page of the travel section in the Sunday paper. Limos *meant* something.

Joanne had to have the biggest, ugliest, most beautiful white Lincoln Continental limousine that couldn't make half the turns on the little streets around her place and the church. Every time the car would stop, an inch from a parked car on either side of a tight street corner, and the driver had to back out of the street again, waving the guy in the car behind him and the one behind him to move out, Joanne squealed in ecstasy and dug her long artificial fingernails into her father's upper arm.

She had to have the car early, had to loop the city in it. Keep the smoked-glass windows up so that people would wonder and try to peer in and guess at the big mucky-muck inside and so what if it didn't happen at that stoplight or the last one or the next one, it'll happen eventually, she thought.

She thought it all through the uneventful ride, paying less and less attention however to the world outside and more to the bar, the TV, the air-conditioning, and the butter-soft white leather upholstery, because it had not, and would not, occur to her that maybe the White Limo didn't mean that anymore.

"Do you *feel* that, Daddy? Feel it, go on. Like you could just poke your little finger right *through* that seat. That's beauty. That's class. Isn't that class, Daddy?"

Sneaky Pete turned away from *The Skins Game* on the little TV, leaned, and kissed Joanne's cheek. Pete, himself a very White Limo kind of guy. "It sure is, sweetheart."

"There they are, there they are. Slow down now," Joanne shouted at the driver. They were approaching Celeste's house, Joanne's hangout starting when she was eleven years old, and ending today.

Jo pressed the button and lowered the window, letting out a long, joyous whoop for The Dogs. In unison, or as close to it as they could manage, Jo's Pack of Dogs all raised their paws limply, casually, coolly, like a lazy group Boy Scout salute. Hell no, they wouldn't be going to no boring stupid church ceremony. Hell yes, they would be going to the reception. And hell right, they were going dressed like that.

Joanne plunked back into her seat, beaming as if she'd just received an ovation, flowers flying, kisses blowing, we love you so, Jo, you are so special. Pete on her one side and

The Dogs on her other still slouched away, mindless of any such moment.

Lois, swollen with the heat, sweat spots blossoming under the arms of her pale-orange dress, was a queen nonetheless. She had seen to that during the arduous week before The Day. Electrolysis to tame the wispy mustache and downy sideburns that really didn't offend anyone but herself. Mud treatment and collagen cream to try and fill the crevices that had been lately cutting like the Colorado River through her tired face. And a fresh perm even though she'd gotten one only two weeks before. "Look at me, Jo," she said on Thursday when she came home from the hairdresser. She balanced a thick Danielle Steel paperback way up high on top of her head, the hair so tight it didn't give at all. Joanne laughed silly and Lois laughed sillier, the first time they did that together, or separately either, in a long time. If they had ever done it all.

Actually, the heat and ungodly humidity were kind to Lois, puffing her face just enough to soften those lines naturally, giving her cheeks a fresh pink that made her look like a happy girl under her new curls. A big colorized Shirley Temple was who she looked like, and Sneaky Pete told her so.

"You look like Shirley Temple, babe," he said into her ear as he whirled her, mid tempo and graceful, from one corner of the dance floor to another. Somewhere, Pete had picked up ballroom dancing.

Lois pulled away from him. He pulled her back. "It's a *com*pliment, Lois, Jesus. I tell ya, every time I laid eyes on that Temple chick, dancing so sassy with that big ol' Bill Robinson, I tell ya, she made me *wild*."

Lois slapped him on the shoulder and giggled, finding the compliment buried in Pete's words the way she always could. "And you look like one of the Beach Boys," she said, referring to Pete's third-degree Florida tan, his floral shirt open to the sternum to display a bouquet of silver hairs, and his white pants. He beamed. He didn't have to look too hard to find the compliment in the words. To Pete that *was* a big compliment.

"You make a great bride muthuh, Lois," he said quietly into her ear. He started singing along with the music.

> *"Waltzing Matilda, Waltzing Matilda*
> *You'll come a-waltzing Matilda, with me."*

Tink tink tink, klink klink klink klink went the spoons against the sides of the wineglasses, and the happy couple kissed. They tinked again, they kissed again. Seemed like it was going to happen a hundred thousand times, with Jo and Gus happy to oblige every time. Too happy, almost, obliging to the point of soft porn, exposing enough tongue and passion right up there on their little stage to embarrass everyone in the room who wasn't fried. Which wasn't too many.

"Buy him a drink, Gus," Joanne would say, pointing out someone who meant nothing to her. "And that one. Buy her a drink too." Gus bought, rolling out the knot of money happily each time, fanning his bride with it first as she tipped her head back in not quite mock ecstasy. "The wad," she called it. "Whip out the wad," she laughed, in love.

Davey lived the day of his sister's wedding through the lens of a camera. "You're the photographer, Davey," Lois said as she draped the strap of the camera around his neck. "It's self-winding, self-loading, auto flash, auto focus. I think you can handle it. Just aim and pull the trigger. Get everything." She stuffed rolls of film in his jacket pockets and pants pockets, making him bulge as if he were wearing saddle bags.

But Davey was happy there. He wasn't happy when Jo told him she was getting married and leaving. Despite the fact that for almost two years now the cycle of month-long screaming matches alternating with super-charged silence between Jo and Lois had driven Davey longer and farther and more often on out of his house, onto his bike, he couldn't bear her leaving. He wasn't happy when the gambling priest spoke of a man shall leave his mother, a woman leave her home, read from Kahlil Gibran, tried to sing "The Wedding Song" a cappella which everyone politely clapped for but Davey didn't because he knew it was stupid. He wasn't happy to see Joanne being strapped into Lois's old gown, sat there in his soaking undershirt as he watched Lois help her daughter with her gobs of makeup, helped her pull and spray her hair till it reached so high the ceiling fan nearly made a flat top out of it. He watched, Davey did, the whole unnatural scene of Lois gingerly, caringly smoothing Jo's edges, packaging her up to deliver her out of there to Gus.

As mother and daughter looked together into the big round mirror of Lois's dresser—Lois crouched behind Jo, who sat and leaned back against her mother—Davey quietly, of course quietly, slipped out to the bathroom and vomited.

He was still a bit jangly when he received the camera. But there, behind that camera, inside it, everyone else locked safely and manageably within the boundaries of the view-finder, *there* Davey was happy.

"Take lots and lots of pictures of my friends, Davey, will ya?" Joanne said as she smiled glowingly, her new husband smiling likewise from behind her with his hands on her abdomen.

"I'll go take 'em right now, Jo," Davey said. Gus walked up and stuck a five-dollar bill in his hand, which Davey stared at through the camera lens. He snapped the picture of Gus's money.

Joanne's friends. The Pack of Dogs, all twelve of them, were the sum total of Joanne's friends. Whether she actually had any friends in the group or not. Good old big stupid old

Phil couldn't make it, being in an army prison in Colorado. Davey went to the bar to take their pictures.

"*Gimp!* Take my picture."

"Bring it here, Davey, take a shot of this," Celeste said, raising her black stretch skirt, bending over and slapping herself on the rear. Davey took the picture.

"Yo, Davey, get this," a fat dog said as he dropped two full whiskey shot glasses into a pint of Guinness and drank the whole thing down. As he slammed the glass down, The Dogs cheered *woo woo woo woo woo*, and a trickle of regurgitated brown-black oil ran out of both corners of the guy's mouth. Davey snapped the picture.

Without talking and without ever pulling his eye from the viewfinder, Davey waved them all in close together for a group shot. The bartender, piling drinks behind them non-stop like a fire brigade, had to be part of the picture. When they were all pressed together in one sweaty, drooling blob, every Dog at once flipped the camera the bird, smiling cheese but saying, "Eat shit, Joaaaaanne." As he snapped it, Davey already knew it was going to be her favorite.

Davey stopped on the way to the dance floor to take a picture of the young waitress, who smiled carefully while balancing her full tray of empty glasses.

He snapped Joanne dancing, for the fifth time already, with the gambling priest who talked like a machine gun in her ear, laughing hard every few seconds although Joanne only smiled.

He snapped the three tables of Gus's relatives, all dressed in black. Gus said that in his culture black was festive. But they looked, faces too, as if they meant to be at the wake that was happening on the opposite side of the street. Davey shot a whole roll of them, fascinated at the changeless expressions through it all.

Sneaky Pete and Lois were dancing again. They were dancing together almost exclusively now, the string broken only by Pete's trips to the bar to refire Lois's vodka gimlet and his manhattan; or Pete's visits to the DJ's table to request yet another special song. Most of the songs said something about remembering. The good old days. When we were young. You'll always be the one. That sort of thing. Sneaky Sneaky Pete, when he sank his teeth into a vein, he bit hard and he sucked.

He sang softly into her ear:

"*I met my old lover
on the street last night . . .*"

Davey took a picture of Lois, eyes closed tight, resting her head like a baby on Pete's shoulder. Then he turned away fast.

While Lois was dancing with Pete, Joanne was dancing with everybody else. All the mourners from Gus's family. All The Dogs, still grabbing her ass, though now she smacked their hands away. She even danced with Gus once or twice.

"Take this one, Davey. Davey, over here, I just *have* to have a picture of this. Take a bunch." There were fifty people all together at the reception, relatives, party slugs, strangers. The kind of crowd you could assemble simply by throwing open the doors of a K of C, VFW, or Elks hall on any sweaty Sunday, without ever sending invitations. It would have been hard to gather any six of the fifty who all liked one another, and it would be even harder to pick six Joanne honestly liked. But now they were all vital to her happiness. "Oh Davey, Davey, get this one, get this one. *The Girls*, all together for the last time." The girls all laughed drunkenly, hugged and kissed, and Davey recorded it.

When it was time to cut the cake, Davey was perched fifty feet away, by the swinging kitchen door, photographing that waitress every time she came through.

"Daaayyy-veeeee!" the whole crowd seemed to scream at once. Davey ran over and got there just in time to snap the bride and groom smashing squares of yellow sheet cake in each other's faces to the sound of hysterical cheering, and "Pop Goes the Weasel" over the loudspeakers.

The cake was still being sliced up when, after a brief,

teasing pause, the sound system came back up, louder than before, and the dance floor filled to capacity. It was karaoke time, and as the first bass lines of "Brown-Eyed Girl" thundered beneath the floor, there was Sneaky Pete rising above the dancers, microphone in hand, standing on the table.

> *"Sha-la-la-la-la-la-la-la*
> *la-la-te-da . . ."*

Pete sang well, not his first time with a mike in his hand. He pointed right at Lois as he finished, and she melted like she was a teenager again and Pete was all four Beatles. Even though her eyes were actually black, not brown.

After serenading her once more, with "You Are My Sunshine," Pete whispered something to the DJ, slapped a big bill in his hand, and stepped down to claim Lois. The heat and the Pete, the gimlets and the wedding of her daughter and the dreamy music were kneading her down. She was cream when Sneaky Pete scooped her up and danced her tight again. She reeled, he pressed. He sang soft and sweet and blew cool on her arched neck at the same time, to Ray Charles's "You Don't Know Me."

> *"No, you don't know the one*
> *who dreams of you at night . . ."*

Davey watched it, the way the TV host watches animals from the bush on nature programs. He shot. He shot Pete stroking his mother's hair. He shot his mother nuzzling Pete's cheek with her nose and playing lightly with his exposed chest hair. He shot his mother nibbling Pete's trapezoid muscle near his neck, and crying dime-sized tears on the silk floral shirt.

"Forget about them, Davey," Joanne said, yanking him by the sleeve. "Dance with *me*." Joanne walked backward onto the dance floor, tugging Davey, who dragged like a mule.

"I have to take the pictures, Jo," Davey said, shaking his head frantically. "I'm too busy, can't dance, can't dance."

"Stop it," she said, grabbing the camera from around his neck. "And smile for a change, will ya, for Christ's sake." Joanne giggled as she began snapping pictures of Davey.

"Cut it out, Jo," he said, covering his face with his hands, turning sideways, looking down at the floor. "That's enough. Gimme back the camera." While he waited for her to give it back he stood looking at the floor, his hands plunged into his pockets, shifting uncomfortably from foot to foot."

"C'mon, Dave, it's only fair. You're taking everybody else's picture, and nobody's taking yours. When I look back, it'll be like you weren't even here." Davey didn't look up as long as she still held the camera. Joanne stopped giggling, looked at him, frozen stiff in the middle of the floor with people wiggling and singing all around him. She walked up and from her position—six inches shorter then him—stuck her face right in his.

"I ain't ever *seen* a photo of you, have I, Davey?"

Davey shrugged his wide, gangly shoulders.

The camera strap hanging around her neck, Joanne took Davey's face in her hands and turned it up. "Keep it right there," she scolded. She took a few paces backward, during which Davey's chin slowly began sinking again. "Ah. Uh-uh," she called. He straightened up to a dignified, if solemn, pose. She reeled off ten pictures from six different angles, then got a cousin to take the two of them together.

"Now. *Dance* with me," she demanded.

Davey didn't fight this time, because he didn't want to. Even though he had never danced with anyone in his life. It was a slow song and Joanne simply guided him around in a toddling circle while she held him.

"You gonna be all right now, Davey? With me gone, I mean?"

He nodded.

"Sure you are. I just needed to hear it. It's not like you need me anymore anyway, huh? Big sucker that you are now. Huh. Huh?"

He nodded again.

"I'm gonna be just a few blocks away anyhow, and you'll

be there a lot, I know. Anytime you want, in fact. Except call first, okay? So I know you're coming. 'Cause I got a family of my own now, Davey, and I got responsibilities for my own home, understand?" She took Davey's hand and placed it on her puffed belly, guiding his hand in a sweeping circular stroking motion. He let his hand stay there a few seconds, his mouth opening slightly to a little O, his eyes taking the same shape. Abruptly, he pulled his hand back.

"Ya, you understand," she said. "Hey, Lois will probably relax, now that I'm gone. She'll be a pussycat, start babying you up all over the place, you being her only baby bird left. It'll be great for you, for everybody, right?"

"Yo sport, can I cut in?" Gus was standing there smiling his sleepy smile. Davey looked at him uncomprehendingly. He held Joanne tighter and continued to turn with her.

"Davey, I really should dance with my husband some," Jo said. She squeezed Davey tight, then gently pushed him away. "Remember, Davey. Anytime you want. Just call first."

Davey stood looking at her, his fingers suddenly scratching and scratching at the seams along the thighs of his pants. He grabbed the camera from the stunned cousin who was still dancing nearby with it hanging around his neck. Before Jo could put her arms around Gus, Davey pressed the shutter release and started taking pictures. Or *picture*, the same one over and over and over, the auto winder advancing the film to the next frame, the flash flashing, strobing, a long series of small lightning bursts popping from Davey's forehead. He stopped when the film ran out. Joanne and Gus went on to dance.

"My baby can *dance?*" Lois gushed as Davey tried to reload. "When did my little one learn how to dance? How come I didn't know my boy could dance? I saw you dancing over there, you . . . dancer."

Davey tried to concentrate on his job, but it didn't matter. Lois seized him in her arms and they were dancing, the camera pressed between them.

"What a wonderful day, Davey. Isn't it a wonderful day?" Lois started welling up again. "Say what you will, your sister and I have certainly had our little moments, but God I love her. And she is the most beautiful bride I have ever seen. And *you* are the most beautiful photographer." Lois gave Davey a big sloppy kiss on the lips, from which he shrank. He didn't like the way she smelled. He didn't like having to hold practically all of her weight as they danced. He didn't like her brand of happiness. Lois tried to pull him closer, but he held her waist stiffly out in front of him, like she was a basketball he was about to pass off. "Isn't she though, Davey? Doesn't Jo look radiant?"

"It must be that magical dress," Pete said, stepping up behind Davey. Lois reached over Davey's shoulder and took her drink. With his newly free hand, Pete clapped his son on the neck. "Your mother looked like a thunderbird in that dress, kid. Put both my eyeballs out, no kidding." Pete squeezed the muscles in Davey's neck, which were so stiff it felt as if he had a wooden coat hanger running under the skin, down his spine and out to his shoulders.

"Jesus, Davey, this is a wedding. Ain't ya havin' any fun?"

Davey wormed out of his father's grip, pulled away from his mother, who was sipping and let him go. "Ya. I'm doin' okay."

"Here," Sneaky Pete said, extending his manhattan glass. "Have a splash, why don'tcha. You're all knotted up."

Lois laughed, slapping Pete playfully on the arm. Davey looked only at the glass. It looked warm and friendly, reddish amber, with a cherry in it. He took a sip. Without asking, he took another one. The warmth that flowed down his throat, then spread like a sunburst in his belly, felt nothing but nice. He even liked the taste.

"Is this mine?" Davey said, nodding at the glass in his hand.

"From me to you," Pete said with a broad toothy smile.

"You watch yourself now, Davey," Lois said, as close as she could manage to motherly. Then she and Pete twirled off.

Davey drank the whole drink right down. The neck muscles loosened, the stomach fluttered again, so sweet a feeling in a place he usually didn't feel. He loaded his camera and hunted down the waitress.

He found her coming out of the ladies' room. She smiled for him one more time, so generous with her dandelion face. Then she walked up to him.

"Don't you think you have enough of those now?"

Davey shivered with the sound of her voice. A little voice, much younger than she must have been. A voice that didn't sound so wrong next to his own young voice.

"WWWWill you dance with me?" Davey said, feeling the coat hanger being yanked up in his shoulders again.

The waitress tilted her head sideways, the break-my-heart tilt that means love, or pity, or confusion. Please don't do that, he thought, putting a hand on his jumping belly to quiet it.

"You're very sweet," she said, and stroked his cheek. "I have to get back to work now."

He watched her walk away, her powder-blue skirt swishing with the motion of a fish tail in the water. He closed his eyes, closed them tight enough and long enough to give himself a headache, unless it was the manhattan. He wanted another one, even if it did hurt his head. He didn't open his eyes until another waitress, not *his* waitress, bumped him and said an excuse me that sounded a lot like get the hell out of the way boy. He climbed up on a speaker set up at the back of the hall, pulled the camera up to his face and kept it there. Joanne and Gus had changed into their going-away outfits and were saying good-bye to all the guests as they gathered in a huge circle around them.

Davey snapped away, picture after picture, from much too far away for any of the pictures to show anything but little nobody people.

FOR THE GOOD TIMES

Lois was breathless, standing in the doorway. "Davey, got any film left? Take our picture some more. Take it, will ya?" She threw her arm around Sneaky Pete again. Davey shot, again.

The two of them mugged like raggedy teenagers squeezed into a three-for-a-buck black-and-white-photo booth, pressing their cheeks together as they both stared out at Davey and said cheese. Kissing. Lois pushing some hair off of Pete's sun-wrinkled forehead. Pete pretending to bounce her perm-sprung head like a basketball.

"Isn't it dreamy," Lois said, falling back on the sofa after Davey had *finally* shot the last of the film. "I mean dreamy. Y'know, dream*like*. Like the biggest dream ever."

"Ya, it's kinda dreamy," Davey said, counting up his little

canisters of film, piling the twelve of them into a pyramid on the coffee table. Pete fooled with the stereo in the corner.

"Joanne is safely married to that nice man with a good job, it was such a beautiful time, and now . . ."

"Now . . . here you go," Sneaky Pete said, slipping into the spot next to her on the couch and slipping a glass of wine into her hand. Pete had put a scratchy record on the turntable. Even though he gave her a CD player for one of her birthdays, she never used it. She said she liked to hear the scratches on the albums, that the scratches made her feel like she was alive when the music played, that she somehow existed. Otherwise the music would make her disappear.

She smiled and clinked glasses with Pete, took a sip. "Oh, Jim Reeeeves," Lois cooed at the singer Pete selected. She swayed to the soft crooning as she spoke. "Just when I thought the house was going to be empty . . ."

Empty, Davey thought.

". . . Suddenly, poof, one gone, another returned. What do you think of that, Davey? I must be living right or something, to have such luck."

Davey had no idea what he thought of that. He looked at Pete, who pulled Lois in tighter. Lois lay with her head in Pete's lap. "We'll see how it goes," Pete said evenly to Davey. Pete could always play Lois like a rag doll, but he knew he had to deliver the straight goods to Davey. "That's all I can tell ya, Davey, okay?"

"Okay," Davey said, finally, finally, finally, at nearly midnight of a long, supposedly joyous day, finally smiling. He wasn't like his mother. A tiny spit of real hope made Davey a lot happier than all the sweet singsong in the world.

As Davey headed off to bed, Pete was working Lois up again, singing along with record. Davey looked back over his shoulder to see his father gently stroking his mother's ear as she lay there purring. Pete looked like a content, real guy, kind of like a husband, or a father. Not like a guy who stuck his thumbs in somebody's eyes. And not sneaky. He loved what he was doing to Lois as much as she loved having it done.

He sang.

*"And make believe you love me
one more time . . ."*

Davey heard many noises he didn't want to hear during the night. The rain on the window was not one of them—it was actually soothing and distracting from the moans and giggles and sudden thrashes coming from the other side of the wall in Lois's room. He made up his mind to move one door down, into Joanne's room, tomorrow. But the noise sounded pleasant, at least. Sounded as if his mother were happy, even if it was in a vague, fragile, sticky sickening kind of a way he didn't quite appreciate. So that was all right with

Davey. If Lois was happy, and if Joanne was happy, Davey could be happy about it. He covered his head with his pillow and blankets and tried to sleep.

It was early when he got up, and he hadn't slept much, but he couldn't stay in bed anymore. He went into the living room and flipped on the TV. He watched the old clay character shows that were always on Sunday mornings, *Gumby* and *Davey and Goliath*. He watched Catholic Mass in Spanish. He watched a knee replacement operation straight through on the medical channel without flinching. By seven o'clock it got boring, even for him, so he got busy moving. He trucked all his clothes down the hall, putting them in the closet and dresser drawers in Jo's room. He tacked his *E.T.* poster to the wall. He brought down all his bedding and made his new bed.

Still there was nothing happening in the house, so Davey made himself some frozen waffles and watched some more TV. He turned off the stereo, which had been on all night and was hot when he touched the top of it. He picked up the wineglasses and coats that had been dropped, washed a few dishes, then stood in the middle of the kitchen with his hands on his hips.

Silence. While it had most definitely never bothered him before, it was chewing at him this morning. But that was no reason to go waking them up. So, despite the rain that was still falling steadily, he went for a bike ride.

He thought he would ride out to the quarry, where he was *sure* to have the place to himself now. He could give a yell across, test out how it carried in the rain, and ride home again. That would be a decent stretch of pumping and would eat up enough time for his parents—he used the word, in his head, and it jarred him—to wake up. But not halfway there the rain bore down on him, he felt a slim stripe of mud being slung up on his back by the tire tread, his light clothes were soaked through, and the big drops were hitting his matted head so that he felt bald.

Davey turned off from his intended route. Where he turned into was the Greyhound station. He stopped and stared, as he always did. He looked at the people who came to drop friends and family at the station for a long trip maybe to college or the army or a new job in another city or just for a cheap vacation that started so early on a Sunday morning that there *were* no arrivals to look at, only departures. Almost everyone cried, he noticed, when they put somebody on a Greyhound bus very early on a Sunday morning. It made him sad, but he didn't want to cry and he didn't want to make them feel better, he wanted to *watch*. He saw other people who just put themselves on the bus and nobody cried about it 'cause nobody knew. He saw other people who sat on benches or floors or curbs and didn't look like they were getting on any buses going to any place. He saw an old old woman wearing a hat that was shaped like a short flour canister with a spray of forget-me-nots sprouting out of the top. A tiny bent thing all pink—makeup, skirt, jacket, blouse, gloves—and breakable enough that she shouldn't be getting on any big nasty bus. But the driver boosted her up, her cloppy black shoes pausing so neatly together on each step, and she was off to Syracuse or Montpelier. He saw people waiting for buses, at the end or the middle of long waits, sleeping on luggage or pacing around, drinking coffee, reading schedules. One of the sidewalk people interrupted Davey in his watching, waving him over. "Kid, kid, kid, c'mere a minute. No no, don't look like that, I ain't gonna pull nothin', I just want to talk." Davey wanted to be home more than before. He pedaled his hardest away from the station, the front wheel of the mountain bike lifting a foot off the ground.

It was the same silence as before when Davey returned, but now he was drenched to the marrow, so it was different. He was better, he was home, and home had become a better thing somehow since he got wet. He could wait. He toweled off, dropped onto the couch, and fell asleep still mostly soaked in front of the TV.

It was almost one in the afternoon when he woke up. And he found himself alone again. Finally, rested and strong and anxious to get on with it, with the whole new thing, he got up the nerve to go to the door and knock. He appreciated that they had had a long, hard-drinking day, but this was enough.

There was no answer to the first knock. There was no answer to the second knock. He didn't wait for an answer to the third, just pushed the door open and knocked simultaneously.

Davey took two steps into the room and stopped. Lois was awake. Her nose was red, her eyes were red, her cheeks, the area between her top lip and her nose, all red, bright, and raw as if she'd been hanging over a boiling pot. Lois was staring blankly at Davey, through him. She hadn't turned as he walked in, she was already staring and had been for hours, and he just stepped into the spot. Lois was alone again.

Davey backed out of the room. He was joyed to find one of his favorite episodes of *Doctor Who* starting up on the sci-fi channel.

LESSA LESTER

I'm on my bike now but it hardly feels like it. Yesterday I was on my bike and I was right here at this spot at this time of day but at that time it *felt* like it. Not like now. The hotness was gone the regular cool was in my thoughts were coming I could sort them I could speak them even and I pedaled and when Lester talked I knew everything. I told him and he told me just like a couple of friends are supposed to tell and so they can understand.

I told my friend Lester about my baby Dennis and how I missed him how I wasn't there with him enough lately how I was gonna maybe have to spend less time with him my friend Lester so my baby Dennis could have me for him like the way he needs.

My friend Lester told me about how he understood perfectly because he had several sparklin' babies he called them of his own scattered around the coast he would like to be spending more time with them too but there are demands on a man demands for providing for the rest and also that with the different babies in the different cities with the different mothers that maybe don't like each other all too much and that maybe don't even like himself Lester all too much these days reunionin' with 'em all can be a hairy deal that hurts more than helps anybody. I could understand that. When Lester told me.

He said he didn't like everything about what all he had to do to get by but there was prices you paid for things steal sometime here to make some money there take a little risk now to buy yourself a little relax later on in life. Gypsy boy I'll tell ya he said to me because he was the one who named me that Gypsy Davey in the first place Gypsy boy I'll tell ya he said I'm a decent man in an indecent business but still and never forget it a decent man that they cannot change not them on this side can change it and neither them on th'other. I do what I gotta do to get what I gotta get he said but I will be through with it all one day when I am still a young man. See I never young Gypsy when I was a young Gypsy like yourself I never liked not no nothin' 'bout myself not a thing and that's the truth. But I always figured figured and figured that if I only had me some money that all that would be different. Well now I got it. And it ain't no different.

So he said so I gotta get outta this here ugly thing I'm into and get after chasin' away that thing whatever it is, however I gotta chase it. Might be a God thing I gotta get into he said but I don't think so.

That was yesterday. Today I'm back but Lester isn't here. I ride to his spot and there's some other guy standing there with a jacket on all black and satin like Lester's but on the back it says Lester . . . Not. A joke I think it is. I know him one of Lester's boys this guy and he sees me riding and riding in a circle looking for my friend Lester like I always do and he talks to me saying yo junior Gypsy boy you looking for your big ol' Lester buddy well they he be and he points to a spot in the gutter where Lester's white Mustang is supposed to be parked but instead today there is a big half-erased white chalk drawing of a big man in the gutter shaped like he's flying like Superman only with just one arm stretched out ahead of him and the other arm pressed down against his side and big red stain maybe Superman's cape in the middle of it.

They's a lot lessa Lesta then they was yesta-day he says laughs to me making his two friends laugh too who are just waiting there against the wall behind him the same as he waited behind my friend Lester all the time up till yesterday. And maybe they oughta be lessa *you* too little Gypsy Davey boy never did like your stupid bike ridin' shiny ass round here no how. I don't want to leave even though it scares me plenty his words but I don't want to. I ride and I ride and I ride up and down that little patch of the street past the street picture of my friend Lester then past it the other way looking at him reconstructing him putting his face back in the picture but they edge closer to me closer again till I can feel the mean breathing and I have no choice except to get away like they want me to. So's why I'm on my bike but it doesn't feel like it this time the cool not coming the hotness not leaving. Pump as hard as I can to get there but I never get there all I get is away away from my friend I talked to that I can't talk to anymore away from the place I used to go that I can't go to anymore.

GOIN' WHERE THE WATER TASTES LIKE WINE

"Should you be doin' that, Jo?"

"Shut up, Davey, all right?"

"It's just that I heard you weren't supposed to do that, when you're, y'know doing that feeding stuff with a new baby."

Joanne took a hard pull on the last of a roach she sifted out of her Holiday Inn ashtray. The baby took a pull at her breast. Joanne held her breath, squinted, blew it out. "Shut up, Davey."

". . . that it does something to them, to their heads, if you do that kind of thing when they're still having the milk."

Again she inhaled while he spoke, this time holding the smoke longer, letting it float to the top of her sinuses like the smoke hovering around the ceiling in a badly ventilated bar.

She blew it out slowly through her nose into Davey's eyes.

"Grab me the photo album over there," she said as he rubbed the burn out of his eyes with the heels of his hands. Davey retrieved the album from the top of the TV and sat back down on the Herculon sofa next to her. Immediately, Joanne pulled the baby off of her breast and stuck him, crying and rooting around desperately for more, into Davey's hands.

Davey bounced the baby Dennis up and down on his knee, then stood and walked him around, still bouncing as he walked. In a few minutes the baby was asleep, sucking on Davey's neck.

"Put him down," Joanne said without looking up from the pictures but pointing to Dennis's room.

When Davey reentered the room, he stood over Jo, who finally looked up. "How come your eyes are black?" he said.

"They're not black. Go in the kitchen and get us a couple of glasses of wine."

Davey returned with two heavy goblets with Budweiser printed on the sides and black red wine brimming over the top. They took big gulps. As she flipped open the album, Joanne simultaneously started the video with the remote control. The wedding video.

"Did he hit you?" Davey said.

Joanne didn't even look up from the photos. "We been married for practically a friggin' year. Gus doesn't care enough anymore to beat me up. I just don't sleep so good, that's all that's wrong with my eyes."

"They look darker than just—"

"Don't look at me anymore, Davey!" Joanne yelled, stabbing Davey in the chest with her fingernail. "Not at me, at the *pic*tures. Get it? Don't-look-at-*me*. Look at the *pic*tures, or go home. I wanna look at my *pic*tures now." She took a drink. Davey took a drink. They looked at the pictures.

"Was I beautiful, Davey?"

"Uh-huh."

"*Day*-vey. I mean, was I *beautiful?*"

"Jo, I don't even know how to say it, you looked so good. I took a hundred pictures of you."

"Ya, but you took about two hundred of that goddamn slutty waitress. What was the deal with her anyway, Davey?"

"Nothin'."

"What, nothin'? Tell me."

"Nothin' nothin'."

"You get anything off her?"

"I'm goin' home, Jo."

Davey stood to go and Joanne tugged him hard back down to the sofa, suddenly very afraid that he would leave.

"Okay, Davey, I'll leave it alone."

There was a long silence as Joanne slowly flipped one page, then another, of the book, then they both looked up to view a slice of the video provided by Happily Ever After Videographers. There was the cake. There was Gus's uncle proposing the toast to his new in-laws, however he figured that. There were The Dogs making one truly embarrassing human pyramid in front of the bar, boys on top, girls on the bottom.

"God, they're great. Ain't they great, Davey?"

"I don't know if they're great, Jo. Maybe, I guess. A lot of them threw up after you left without even going to the bathroom and then they just stood there in the middle of it and asked for more drinks. One of 'em asked me to take a picture of it. I didn't like it too much."

"Hah!" Joanne snorted. "Characters. I gotta get in touch with them again. Except that Celeste. Look at her, how fat she got. She's a big pig."

"Well it wouldn't be too hard to get in touch with them. They're still on the porch."

"I will." Joanne looked down and started rubbing her soft thigh, larger now than it was when she gave birth. "I'll be back, y'know, Davey. I'm only seventeen years old, for Christ's sake. I got a long way to go yet."

"Seventeen and a half."

"Fill us up, Davey," Jo snapped, sticking her empty glass in his hand. He went and filled it, and when he returned Jo was giggling at the part of the video that makes her giggle every time they watch it together, which is about every two weeks.

She freezes the frame with the remote. Watches it play in reverse. Plays it forward again. On the screen, Lois carries on a conversation with the priest, while Sneaky Pete from behind gratuitously tongues her ear and strokes her breasts.

"He is *so* cute. God, he still loves her, old dishrag that she is. That's love, Davey, y'know it? That's love. That's it, that's the *thing*."

Davey looked down, at the album. He could never look at that sequence.

"And the priest, he loved it too. He's a diddler. Look at him talking on and on like he doesn't know what's happening, his hands wigglin' around in his pockets lookin' for change for a goddamn half hour." Joanne launched into a fit of hysterics, spilling wine in the lap of her gray sweatpants. "Wow. Was that a great day, or *what*?"

From the other room, the baby cried. Davey sprang up to get him.

"Shit," Joanne said, punching the seat cushion. "Let him cry a little. He needs to cry a little. It's supposed to be good for their lungs."

Davey ignored her and brought Dennis into the room. When the baby saw his mother, he started lunging for her.

"Ya, ya, ya," she sighed, throwing open her shirt. "All he wants to do is fuckin' eat." She looked down at the top of the baby's head, the still-open soft spot throbbing in her direction.

"Well get your fill, boy, 'cause this is last call. He's seven months old already, he doesn't need this anymore. And to tell you the goddamn truth, it used to be cute, and it gave me kind of a buzz, but I'm tired as hell of it. Tomorrow he stops, that's it."

"Where's Gus?" Davey said, staring at that same soft spot on the baby's head.

"Gussie's at his mommy's house, in Greece. Again. Same one we spent our honeymoon in with his fifty fucking relatives." She stuck her finger in her mouth and made a gagging sound. "Seems his Yaya went to bed and bumped her head and couldn't get up in the mornin'."

"His grandmother's *dead*, Jo?"

"How the hell do I know. All I know is he's not here. But he's *never* here, which is okay because even when he's *there* he sends me the money *here*, so, I got no complaints."

On the video, Jo and Gus are waving good-bye to the circle of well-wishers, circling again, then once more. Jo flipped her book to the still pictures of the same scene, following along like a children's readalong tape, like she always does. "That was so clever of you, Davey, the way you took those pictures from so far away, to show that we were going so far away. Real artsy. I think maybe you got a gift or somethin', for this photography thing. You might be somebody with it."

Davey stood up to go as Jo rushed the video back to the tongue scene. "You can finish my wine, Jo," he said, sliding his glass toward her over the walnut-veneer coffee table.

Jo popped up out of her seat, pressing the baby against her as he continued feeding. "Already, Davey?" Her voice shook. "I thought we'd have some lunch. I can make you lunch. I got macaroni and cheese. Okay? Sit back down."

Davey just had to move, to put his feet on the pedals and pump madly until the wine seeped out his pores and rolled down his face and the wind froze it there. "I gotta go, Jo."

"Okay," she said, walking him to the door. "But you come back right away. Tomorrow, if you want, okay?"

Davey smiled, a bit too sweetly maybe, making her feel like the little one. Joanne straightened up, took a brief grab at the old cat cool. "But call first. You gotta call first before you come here."

Davey nodded. Jo stood in the doorway, holding the baby around the shoulder blades, almost by the neck, as the rest of the little body dangled below like a windless wind sock.

"Remember all the calls I used to get at the house, Davey? Remember all the calls, the crazy phone ringing all day and all night and Lois screaming me out and pissed off and jealous? Remember the sound of that phone goin' all the time?"

Jo hardly seemed to notice Davey backing down the stairs with his bike over his shoulder, didn't seem to hear him tell her that he did remember, even if he wasn't quite sure that he did.

GREAT THINGS IN CONVERTIBLES

Sneaky Pete stopped sending money. That wasn't all that unusual. He stopped sending his monthly money every two months or so, but he always started back up again and usually made up the difference. Lois lived and died with those payments, but she always survived because she knew they'd get there eventually. But this time, when it reached three consecutive dry months, she had to start something. She started a correspondence.

"I have a child here" was the gist of the first letter.

"Get a job" was the gist of the reply.

"I'll get a *mouthpiece*" was the return.

"You better get a *bloodhound*," Pete answered, "'cause I'll be gone like smoke."

This went on through four, five, and six penniless months, and as her pitch rose in the letters, it crashed in person. Without her monthly boost, Lois slowed down. Her perm grew out to look like an SOS pad that had been used to scrub a thousand pots, frayed, burned, and tin gray. She couldn't go out where the action was so much, so she stayed at home, watching TV with Davey and composing letters.

"I'm going to kill you, Peter. I'll walk to Florida if I have to and when I get there I'm going to sink my claws so far into your throat they're going to come out your ears. I mean this. You are a dead snake."

Pete wrote promptly back. "Lois, if you will call me on the phone and talk to me like that for just two minutes, I promise I'll pay you all your money and more. I love you."

Lois showed the letters to Davey. "Your father is a very sick man. And he's a deadbeat. I'm going to put him in jail, Davey. I hope you understand that."

Davey nodded, returned the letters to her. "I'd do it," he said, then went to the kitchen to make them the macaroni and cheese they ate every night for supper.

For the first time, men started actually coming to the house. Sometimes Lois brought them back with her from the bar. Other times they took her out for dinner and came back later toting a couple of bottles of wine. If it was early, Davey hopped on his bike and came back quietly in the night. If it was a dinner date, he just made sure to be in bed when they got back.

Lois came bouncing through the door with Leo on her

arm one afternoon while Davey was stirring the macaroni.

"Oh put that nonsense away for tonight," Lois said. "Here." She stuck a dripping basket of buffalo wings in his hands. "Leo here insisted on buying tonight."

Davey turned off the burner, placed the pan directly into the refrigerator for when his mother would undoubtedly be rooting for it in the morning. He sat down and started into his chicken while Lois went into the bathroom to reapply a generous layer of makeup—where does the old makeup go? he wondered—and Leo yanked the cork out of one of the two bottles he'd bagged in.

Davey's mouth was full when Leo placed a full milk glass of wine on the table. Davey instinctively grabbed it.

"Are you supposed to have this?" Leo asked politely.

Davey nodded. "Ya, I'm supposed to have it."

"You seem like a good kind of kid," Leo said, filling two more glasses of different sizes, then sitting across from Davey. "Your sister, from when I met her that time, she seemed like a fresh one. But you, you seem like a good kind of kid."

"I am," Davey said. "I'm the best kind."

"Ta-daaa," Lois sang as she reentered the kitchen. Leo turned toward her, bunched his fingertips together, and kissed them like she was food, spraying the whole mess at her. Davey ate.

"Thank you, thank you, thank you," she said and clanked

glasses with both of her gentlemen. "An embarrassment of riches," she said. Her hair was still matted with water on top from where she had tried again to smooth the huge lump that was always there in the wake of the permanent.

"Thanks for the food, Leo," Davey said, standing and gulping the last of his second glass of wine. "I'm gonna go for a little ride now, Ma. I'll see you later."

"Okay, sweetie," Lois said, giving him a big dramatic kiss on the cheek, leaving a red and pink and cream-colored makeup bruise over half his face.

Two glasses of wine, different from one glass of wine, made Davey do things. He rode, of course.

He rode as fast as he could. He rode down the long steep hill that led into the big intersection where even if you do have the light your way you stop because there isn't any respect for that light. As he neared the light he heard it, heard the bad muffler, the accelerator push as the light turned yellow. Davey heard it, and he pedaled harder because he could tell that the car was ahead of him and might pass harmlessly through before he got there. He pushed, to twenty, thirty miles per hour, baring his teeth into the wind he was creating for himself. He leaned, an aerodynamic bullet, slicing that wind to get there, and when he hit the bottom, he closed his eyes. He straightened up and took his hands off his handlebars.

The big old Cadillac rocked him as it thundered past two

feet behind Davey's rear wheel, the driver having no more intention of stopping, slowing, or swerving than Davey had.

Davey laughed out loud as he crossed out of the intersection, opening his eyes now but still riding no hands, the hands rubbing excitedly up and down over his own chest.

He rode to Jo's house, didn't even wake her as she slept on the sofa. He strolled right by her, walked into baby Dennis's room, stood there looking at the body curled up in a ball, wearing only a diaper. He pulled a blanket up over him, kissed him, and walked out again.

He rode to the place he wasn't supposed to ride to. He visited the man who stood in dead Lester's shoeprints. The man told him he still didn't like his shiny ass; Davey said he understood. The man gave Davey the five dollars and the address and Davey delivered. Then Davey took his five dollars over to the next block and handed it to the big lady who hugged him and told him that she loved him. She took him into the vestibule, told him to hush his jumpin' heart, and let him touch her. She gave him a kiss and a slab of jalapeño corn bread and told him again that she loved him.

Davey rode to the quarry, did not call out for fear of attracting anybody and giving up his solitude. He took off his clothes and swam in the frigid water, a quarter mile to the opposite side, and back, with a ten-minute pause in the dead center to tread water and bob like he was nothing but a head in the great wide open. He put his clothes on his dripping body, then finally called out, his answer coming back to him in a wave, some of it words, some of it not quite words but all of it Davey, from the inside of him.

It was after midnight when Davey stepped back into the house, clammy and goose-pimpled, the damp clothes puckering all over his long bones. He paused in the living-room doorway to look at Leo's shirt thrown over the back of the couch, his black Bostonian shoes on the floor next to Lois's shoes.

Then, without warning, Leo was there, standing side by side with Davey, the two of them staring at the shoes. Davey glanced sideways, down at Leo. He was rounder and shorter in his tank-top T-shirt and no shoes.

"So, how was *your* night?" Leo said, wise-guy words, but not a wise-guy attitude.

"Good," Davey said, and when Leo went to say more, he cut him off. "But I don't care how yours was."

Leo shut his mouth and nodded. He collected his stuff under Davey's mute supervision, they shook hands, and he left.

In the morning, Lois was eating the macaroni and cheese out of the pan with a big wooden spoon while Davey watched TV. It was sunny out and when it was sunny Lois liked to spend the morning—the entire morning—in the window seat with her back to the world, her head leaning against the pane. When it was rainy, she liked to spend the morning in the same window seat but turned around, staring at the rain. Now she stared at Davey, as much as her red-rimmed eyes were actually focused.

Slight as it was compared to the TV noise, when the doorknob clicked in the front hall both Davey's and Lois's heads snapped to it. Why would the door ever open? They were both here already.

Sneaky Pete strolled in, took his seat next to Davey on the couch, with his arm around him, and started leafing through the two-month-old *TV Guide*. "Breakfast ready, hon?" he said, smiling.

For a few seconds nobody moved. Everybody gawked. They waited for it to go away. Lois figured it was just a little leftover grape. After all how many times had she conjured this scene under the influence? Davey, for his part, had reached the point where he could believe absolutely anything and absolutely nothing. If Pete transmogrified into a bat or a vulture or a flying monkey and disappeared out the window, Davey would have turned quietly back to his program.

"You have got brass balls, Pete," Lois said, dropping her pan on the floor.

"Thanks, Lois. You're lookin' kinda metallic yourself."

"Where's my money?"

"Ain't got no money."

"Then what are you doing here?" Lois was now walking, stalking Pete's way.

"It was that last letter of yours, the fresh one. You know, the one with all that physical stuff about the places you were going to put your fist and your foot and all that. Made me *crazy*. I just had to come up."

Lois was standing right in front of Pete now, in her thick gray terry-cloth bathrobe, bare feet, swatches of makeup on her cheek, her chin, her hair. The black eye makeup that was too much when it *was* in place now made her chilling, and the look from inside her was not pro-life. Davey scooted down the couch away from them.

"Where's my fucking money, Peter?"

Pete was coolest, as if having his life threatened was not all that unusual. "This time you don't get a check, Lois. You get *me* instead."

Lois took a step back. She looked at Davey, whose blankness was no help. Then back at Pete. "What does that mean, Pete?"

"Daddy's home," he said, grinning, his hands extended palms up to accept the applause.

"Home? Home where?" she said.

"Home here."

Lois turned to Davey again. "You see, Davey, this is my

curse. My animal magnetism, it makes me attract all kinds of animals." She turned back to Pete. "Get out of here, you pig," she said, then stomped back to her window seat, scooping up her bucket of macaroni on the way.

Sneaky Pete got up and slowly walked to the stereo. He flipped it on, threw "Sinatra at the Sands" on the turntable, and strolled Lois's way.

"Forget it," she said, menacing him with her wooden spoon.

When he reached her, she didn't hit him. He kissed her on top of her greasy head. "Look," he said, pointing out the window. Lois turned around, kneeling in the chair, as Pete pointed out an antique showroom-new sea-green 1960 Cadillac El Dorado convertible at the curb.

Pete got very humble. As Sinatra crooned "It Was a Very Good Year" for a backdrop, Pete told her, "*That* is where your money for the past few months went—I was savin' up. I bought it for you. I mean, I'll drive it and it's registered to me, but it's for you."

Lois could not stop looking at the car, first smiling, then giggling. "It is the single most beautiful thing I ever saw," she said. She started crying. "You really staying, Pete? I mean, really?"

"Really. I thought about it long, Lo, and I figured I was just kiddin' myself these last years, that maybe I'm not the kinda guy who should be alone. I decided I could be *great*, livin' back here. What I need in my life are witnesses. As long as I got witnesses I can behave."

"Davey," Lois squealed, "you have to come see this."

Davey came to the window and looked down at the glimmering machine, its new green leather interior open to the sunlight.

"It's a nice car, Ma," Davey said.

She took both of Davey's hands in hers and squeezed, bouncing up and down. "God, Davey, you don't know. This is a sign. This is bigger than all of us and bigger than that car down there—"

"Which is pretty goddamn big." Pete was happy to cut in.

"Davey, it's like, great things have always happened to me in convertibles. That's all I can say."

Pete laughed out loud. Davey looked again out at the El Dorado for some sign of its magic life.

"And look at that pretty Florida license plate," Lois said. "I always said it was the prettiest of all license plates. It just says so much, it's so tropical and glamourous and nice." She turned to Pete abruptly again, turning serious in a blink. "Really this time, Pete? No flitting, no smoke tricks, no scheming?"

Pete shook his head and held up his hands like she'd pulled a gun on him. "This monkey's been chasin' the weasel too long. I'm out."

"Pop goes the weasel," Lois sang, hugging Pete hard

enough to make him cough. "Why don't we go for a ride? Right now. Can we, Pete?"

"Let's do the beach," Pete said. "We'll go to Kelly's and have some fat burgers and onion rings and fried clams and ice cream, and we'll throw the wrappers on the ground and sit in the car and listen to the waves and maybe we'll puke."

Lois slapped Pete on the arm and laughed uncontrollably. "I can't wait. Let's go right now. I'll go just like I am." She ran to the front door.

"Whoa, whoa, whoa," Pete said. "Lois, come back here. Honey, if I'm gonna be here, you can't go around looking like *that*. The beach'll wait. Get yourself a shower. Burn the bathrobe. Slap on some makeup. Put on some heels and some shorts. I'll be waiting."

"I'll be five minutes," Lois said.

"Take twenty," Pete said as he headed for the kitchen. "Got a beer, Lo?"

She called from the bathroom. "There might be one in the vegetable drawer."

Pete found the beer, cracked it open, and when he turned around Davey was right there.

"So, guy," Pete said, much less confident than the tone he used with Lois. He still knew who was who. "You happy to see me?"

"I am, Dad."

"I didn't bring you nothin' this time."

"I don't want nothin'."

"Pretty soon, though, I'll have myself established up here again, I'll have something to give ya."

Davey leaned very close to Pete, closer than Davey usually got with people. "You just give my something to Ma, okay? Give *all* my somethings to Ma."

Pete shied a bit, nodded, squinted that he received the message clearly.

"Davey," Pete said after a long suck on the Pabst Blue Ribbon can, "you believe me? About everything?"

"Ya. I believe you. You're my dad."

Pete smiled, more tentatively this time. He couldn't quite read his boy this time the way he would have liked, so he couldn't produce the home-run smile.

"Davey, you gonna come for a ride to the beach with us?"

"Sure. Can my bike fit in the trunk?"

Lois sang in the shower.

> *"When I was twenty-one*
> *It was a very good year . . ."*

Pete flipped Davey the keys to the El Dorado, and Davey brought his bike down as Pete drank his beer.

HYSTERICAL

There are things I know. There aren't a million things I know but there are a few more than people think I know. I know that when Pete lives with us there is music in the house all the time which is a good thing and my mother is laughing all the time when she's not crying which is of course some of the time a good thing because even if he's sneaky Sneaky Pete sure is funny. Hysterical is what Ma says to almost anything he says when the good stuff is happening and there's some money and the fridge is full and the glasses are all full including mine. High-sterical is how she says it.

I know that when Pete is not here it's a different place Ma says she doesn't give a rat's ass and well fuck you anyway and she's not here herself a lot of the time sometimes for a lot of straight days and when she is she hugs her knees and looks out the windows and doesn't take any showers and stares and stares and stares and only eats when I make macaroni and cheese and put it right in her mouth for her. Dual citizenship is what she says Pete has living in Florida whenever it's cold up here which means he's never here after November or before May which means I still never seen the guy on a Christmas even though he sends me stuff great stuff stuff you wouldn't believe stuff like cameras and radios Walkmans and Watchmans that go with me so I can see TV if I want anywhere even on my bike which made me crash bounce off a car and crack my brains open onto the street and so I don't do anymore. I got home all right walking instead of riding 'cause I couldn't y'know ride sat in front of the TV sometimes awake sometimes asleep for I guess a couple of hours and really soaking up a whole bath towel with my blood and brains all over it before Ma came home and made me figure that I should have got myself to the damn hospital instead of sitting in front of the tube like a damn lame-o and she supposes that maybe I did leave some of my brains on the curbstone.

The thing about that is I get things lots of things when Sneaky Pete isn't there and I don't get a whole lot of anything when he is there.

I know that when it rains out I have to bring something into the bedroom coffee and English muffin into the bedroom and juice and turn on the music or Ma will not get out of the bed for the cryin' and that once I do that I have to ride direct over Jo's house and do a kind of the same thing only it's bring her a coffee and six different donuts from Dunkies that she eats all by herself and a Bavarian crème for the baby Dennis which when you see him eat it at least when I do is maybe probably the cutest thing you ever saw with the yellow inside and the chocolate outside smeared all over his mouth his eyes his forehead his hair and I almost cry at it which is about the stupidest thing ever because good things don't make you cry so instead I laugh because that's a better thing. I wash his face with a dishcloth that I wet at the sink with warm not hot or cold water and I take my good long time doing the washing because he turns his little face up and closes his eyes tight and he lets me.

I know that I don't tell Jo or Ma that the rain makes Jo look a lot like Ma and Ma look a lot like Jo I don't say it because I don't like screams I don't like slaps and most of all I don't like spitting.

I know that it doesn't matter to anyone even a little bit that I'm the biggest one around here now.

I know that every time I see the baby Dennis I think more and more. I think things people would probably think I shouldn't be thinking but I think I don't care. I think I'm his best friend and we are supposed to be together. I think that the pile of mail that stacks up on the floor by Jo's front door without her opening it that I look at that says Department of Social Services and Urgent and Please Respond Immediately that Jo snatches from me and says cut the shit Davey I know that stuff means something and the something doesn't feel good. I know Jo doesn't answer her phone anymore and that it rings all the time when I'm there and who could it be after all when she was always saying call me call me because nobody was ever calling her. I know that if I come by two days in a row Dennis is wearing the same stuff and smelling the same as he did the day before and that Jo used to let me do all the stuff but now she tells me it's *my* kid you know Davey who the hell do you think you are Davey you think a puny fucking donut every few days makes you the kid's fucking father Davey and if I say there's no shit in his diaper there's no shit in his diaper so get on your silly little bike which by the way looks really stupid now that you're nine feet tall and too big for it just hop on it and pedal to hell trying to tell me I'm not a good fuckin' mother is what she says.

But I know things. I know there's shit in my baby Dennis's diaper I know I'm not going to let it stay there and hurt him I know I can't just keep away and let something bad happen to him I know he needs I know I'm the one.

UNTIL HE COULDN'T SEE IT ANYMORE

Davey was just wheeling around the corner when he saw the big man loading the suitcase into the trunk of his dark-blue retired police car LTD. The car was parked in front of Jo's house, sandwiched tight between two other cars, beside the hydrant. When he recognized the head in the passenger seat of the car as his sister's, he sped up.

The rain was just starting, but it was heavy the way it is early on a summer morning when the sun's trying to heat it up. Davey jumped off the bike while it was still rolling, letting it crash on into the next car without him.

"Who's that?" Davey said evenly, talking to Joanne though the glass, pointing at the man now starting up the LTD. Joanne didn't answer, didn't roll down the window, didn't turn to look at Davey. She held the baby Dennis tight to her and sat stone-faced while he slept in her arms.

"Jo?" Davey said. He held up the bag of donuts. The LTD's muscly engine raced. "Jo?" Davey stood his ground as the car moved slightly up, then back, then up again to try and maneuver out of the space. Davey looked down at the top of the baby's head. "Jo? Jo, you want to leave the baby Dennis here with me while you go out? Open the door. I'll watch the baby."

The car was out of the space and pulling slowly away when Joanne half turned her eyes on Davey.

"Jo? Open the window, huh? Let the baby Dennis just have his Bavarian crème donut. Can he? He likes a Bavarian crème, you know that." Davey trotted alongside the car as it picked up speed, his palm flat on the glass as close to the baby's head as he could get it. "Dennis? Dennis?"

Davey ran his gangly run after the car until he couldn't see it anymore, and for ten minutes after.

LIKE HELL TO PIECES

When I went back and got my bike there were two good things two lucky things which was how I knew everything was going to be okay. The first lucky thing was that after all that time my bike was still there lying in the street the second lucky thing was that there was a rainbow which is supposed to mean that lucky stuff is gonna go your way isn't that what that means? Even if the rainbow was one of them city street rainbows made by the rain falling on the dirty motor oil stain a couple feet from the curb it still was pretty a beautiful rainbow so there's no reason the luck thing shouldn't still be there for me right?

I'll be all right I'll be okay because what it is is I must have been wrong about Jo. Jo must really love the baby Dennis like I thought she didn't because why would she steal him away like that if she didn't. That's love. So they'll be all right he'll be all right and if it hurts me a little bit sometimes and maybe it hurts me a lot other times well that's all right too because now I know that Jo loves the baby Dennis and she's gonna take care of him from now on her and that guy whoever he is.

It only hurts for now anyway then I'll be over it because it's gonna be my own time soon and the baby Dennis he was never really my own baby anyway no matter what craziness I felt about him and that's all past. I can't hardly even remember it in fact is what I'm saying to myself right now.

He had on his hat the yellow round one with the big stitching in it that made his little baby head look like a softball when he wore it. Just like a softball only it was softer even than a softball because his skin and his fuzzy baby hair that still wasn't growing too fast made the baby Dennis's real head feel like flannel when you put your nose or your cheek or your big forehead against it. But with the hat on the yellow hat with the big stitches he did still look like a softball a warm soft softball and even if Joanne didn't have it tied in front like I would have he was still probably okay because it was warm outside that day when he had the hat on and Jo didn't let me say good-bye.

Anyway soon sooner than you think probably because I'm almost a man already I'm gonna have my own find somebody who's gonna love me and we're gonna have some babies and I'm gonna love 'em like hell to pieces like nobody ever loved babies before.

Here's a sneak peek at

little blue lies

little blue lies

CHRIS LYNCH

AUTHOR OF THE NATIONAL BOOK AWARD FINALIST INEXCUSABLE

Oliver loves Junie Blue. That's true. The thing is, pretty much everything else is a lie. Junie and O are both known for their lies—and the only thing that felt true was their relationship. But now Junie Blue has dumped Oliver, and he's miserable. She says they're done, but is she lying?

Junie's father, a toady for One Who Knows—head of an organized crime family—won't tell O where Junie is. When O hears a rumor that Junie has a winning lottery ticket—a ticket that One Who Knows expects to be given—O is determined to come to her rescue. But can O give Junie what she truly needs?

Available from SIMON & SCHUSTER BFYR

The problem, or thrill, depending on how you choose to look at it, was that our relationship was practically *based* on an enthusiastic mendacity. Her nickname for me was Lyin' O'Brien. Mine for her was Sweet Junie Blue Lies.

She told me in one of our earliest conversations that her mother had died in a plane crash. And that she had an airplane tattooed on her hip with her mother's initials on the wings. Then I ran into her at CVS four weeks later, where I was cheerfully introduced to her living, earth-walking mother, as well as her sister, Max, who I had been led to believe was her brother, Max. Oh, not an actual plane crash, she said. That was just a metaphor for the marriage. Then after another six long weeks I finally met Junie's hip. There was, in fact, an airplane tattoo. The origin of the initials changed every time I asked. I stopped asking.

Still, thrill is how I choose to look at it. She made lying exciting, and sporty, and really I picked up the habit only when she got me hooked. It was our bond. Then again, we're not together anymore either, so my assessment could be open to question.

June Blue. A guy does not break up with that name lightly. Or voluntarily, as it happens. I was dumped.

She says that her grandfather is a rabbi in London, and I have no reason to doubt her. I told her my grandfather was a bishop in Waterford, and I have no reason not to believe me, either. I've been to his grave, and his headstone is shaped like one of those hats. There you go.

Right? So if that's not soul-matey enough for you, there's our fathers. No, not "Our Fathers," like that moan prayer they used to push in the church, and which would not ever have crossed Junie Blue's puffy orange lips. Our actual fathers. Mine is a robber baron and hers is—whatcha know?—the regular kind. And don't go thinking I mean "baron," all right, since what in the world would a *regular* baron be like?

And they both sell, among other things, insurance.

Before I met him, she told me her father looked exactly like John F. Kennedy. Then I met him. If you dug Kennedy up today, he'd still be better-looking.

Yet in spite of all that, June and I are as honest as the day is long. Unless you count lying, which, really, nobody does.

Honest day's work/honest day's pay, we have no quarrel with that business at all. She works two jobs too, one having grown out of the other, and both legitimate. She works evening and early morning and weekend hours at the corner-store that is about seven corners away from her house. It's in a neighborhood where all corner-store counters would be bulletproof Plexiglassed from the criminals, but for the fact that all their criminals are *their* criminals. And all of *those* criminals are operating under the benevolent eye of One Who Knows, who does not like his neighborhood being dirtied up by petty crime and unwholesomeness that detracts from his sepia view of life in the microclimate that extends four miles in every direction from his modest not-quite-beachside house. You wind up with kneecap and testicle troubles if you screw with One Who Knows and the sepia view.

Junie's humor, right? It's like this. Everybody knows One Who Knows as One Who Knows, except, when we would talk about him, it bothered her to have to sound so, you know, reverential to the guy. Even though she has met him on many occasions and likes him fine enough, she's got her principles still. The guy even has the tattoo down one forearm, the initials stacked like a totem pole, *OWK*. "Owk," Junie said one day, calling me from the store just after he left. He bought a loaf of Wonder Bread and a whole roll of scratch cards and as usual tipped her with ten of those cards. "I mean, thanks for the cards, *Owk*, but, really, *Owk*? It's not even a word or a decent acronym or anything. It's like you asked an owl, 'Hey, what kinda bird are you,' and just when he goes to tell you,

you punch him in the stomach. That's the noise he would make, '*Owk!*'"

I laughed, like I did almost all the time when she talked, but then, also like usual, I began the reasoning process. "So, nobody asked you to call him that. Just use his proper name. One Who Knows."

"Aw, shit to that. I'm not calling anybody that."

"Why not? It's got a ring. Listen," I said, and ran through the full phrasing several different ways, slow and fast and articulated and mumbled and—

"Hold it," she said.

"What?"

"That last one. Do that last one again."

"As I recall," I said, "it went a little something like this . . ."

"That's it," she said.

What I did was rush the three words together, with an opening flourish and a gentle fade-out at the end. Nice work, but nothing special. I do stuff like that all the time.

"Juan Junose." She said the *J*s making *H* sounds, and I could hear her smiling. She has big pearly teeth with a middle gap you could park a cigarette in, which she does sometimes, and it's heart-flutter stuff. Smoking and hearts, eh?

"Juan?" I said.

"From this point onward. Or, Juanward."

I loved the Spanishness of it. Particularly as our Mr.

Junose is the type of guy who, if he found himself being any kind of Spanish, he'd shoot himself in the face.

"Juan," we said at the same time and in the same key. Soul-matey, right?

We did stuff like that regularly, at least until school finished and we unfortunately did likewise. We graduated a month ago, and everything was sailing along like a happy horny boat like always until we hit the reef. I never saw it coming.

"Why?" I asked, and the only reason I didn't sound like a complete weenie dog was because I was taken so entirely by surprise. Given even just a little bit of advance notice, I would have worked up a whimper that would still be singing today if you walked down to the beach and put a seashell to your ear.

I liked June Blue very much. Still do.

"Because we're not kids anymore, O." She liked to call me O, because it fit so well into most of our conversations. *O, for Christsake . . . O, shut up . . . O, God, put that thing away. There are kids in the park. . . .*

"Yes, we are," I said. "Don't let that graduation thing fool you. We're still kids, and will be for quite some time."

She just shook her head at me sadly from her spot so far away at the other end of the seesaw.

"Your head's going in the wrong direction," I said, suddenly bumping the seesaw up and down frantically, getting her whole self into the proper nodding action.

She giggled gloriously but didn't change her mind. She held fast to the seesaw and to the horrible sad squint that was maiming her features. Confusion and panic ran through me like a fast-acting poison, and so, being a clever guy and quick on my feet, I did something.

See, probably the one bone of contention we ever had in a year and a half of going out was that my folks have money, and so I have money, and her family doesn't have anything like that. A problem for her, but I was always cool and magnanimous with it.

So I did something.

"No," she said. "No. You did not."

"What?" I said, removing my hands from the seesaw so I could make the ineffective pleading gesture to the heavens.

"You did *not* just offer me money to stay with you."

Pleading hands were required to stay where they were. "What? No. It wasn't . . . That's not . . . You just misconstrued . . ."

We had the balance thing going pretty well, considering that I outweigh her by about thirty pounds, but when she flung herself backward to get off the seesaw and out of my life, I dropped like a pre-fledgling baby bird to the ground.

And if one of those nestless, flightless, awkward bundles

of patchy feather and hollow bone had been blown up to adult human size and plunked on the ground at the down end of a seesaw, he would not have looked one chirp more ludicrous than I did at that moment.

But I didn't care about that.

"Junie?" I called desperately.

"If you even dare try to follow me, I'll have your legs broken, O."

And since June Blue is one of those rare people who can say that and actually do that and can do it on speed dial, I just sat with my bruised everything until two seesaw-deprived preschool girls came along and stared me into slouching away home.

Her second job is dog walker. Visitors to the store started asking after she took care of the owner's mutt for a couple of days when he had a couple of toes excommunicated because of diabetes. People in June's neighborhood apparently have diabetes at such a rate that people get toes popped like having bad teeth removed, and word spreads fast when there is a reliable babysitter, window washer, or dog walker around. June is popular, and busy, and one of her sometimes clients is the man himself, Juan, who has the ugliest Boston terrier on earth, with three deep scars across his snout and an ass like a tiny little baboon.

I take walks sometimes. It's not stalking.

I don't take binoculars, or rope, or flowers.

I take hope, best intentions, and, okay, that spicy ginger chewing gum that she loves and you can only get in Chinatown, but that hardly changes anything.

"That tree isn't even wider than you, doofus," she says.

What does one do in this situation? I'm looking a little simple here, skinnying myself behind this immature beech tree diagonally across from the house that June has just stepped out of. I'm not stupid. I know this tree is not adequate for my purpose, but I had my eye on a burly elm only fifteen yards farther, when June and that Airedale with the bad nature stepped out the door a full ten minutes before the usual walking time for a Tuesday.

"I'm not stalking you," I say, still inexplicably remaining there, only partially obscured by the sapling. I may have lost my fastball, lying-wise.

She continues on her appointed round.

"Stalking Archie, then?"

"He's not my type."

"Good. 'Cause he doesn't like you either."

It's true, he doesn't, but more important, what did she mean by that, "doesn't like you, either"? *Either* as in, Archie and I share a mutual animosity? Or she and Archie share a dislike of me? This is the kind of stupid, obsessive thought

I have now? Look what you've done to me, Junie Blue.

"Did you just say you didn't like me?" I say pathetically as she strides down the block and away from me again.

"No," she says. And that's all she says.

"Gum?" I call after her, the pack held aloft like I am the Statue of Liberty's tiny little embarrassing brother.

The high school we went to is often cited in lists as America's finest public school. There is a citywide exam to get in after sixth grade, and I was determined to take it even though the highly rated private school I went to had everything but its own moat. I alarmed my parents both by doing well on the exam and by insisting on going there. Rebellion? No. I'm pretty sure I was intent on meeting a greater variety of girl-folk. There were no Junie Blues in my previous existence, that's for sure.

When June and I were still students there, things were much better. We had two classes together final term, and I tell you what, in those classes I did not learn a money-humping thing.

English and history, and we clung like mutual barnacles to each other's hull for every class, making jokes and talking all manner of nonsense. We had our regular seats, and we would always make plans to meet there, as if there were any mystery at all as to where we were going to sit.

"Back of English," she would say, pointing at me as we

passed in the corridor prior to third period Tuesday and Thursday.

"Wrong side of history," I would say prior to fourth period Wednesday and Friday. It was a favorite term of our history teacher, Mr. Lyons, whom everybody called Jake, and who talked with this fantastic squelch effect like he had a tracheotomy. *You don't want to wind up on the wrong side of history*, Jake would say whenever he was pointing out some of the greatest errors in judgment that hindsight could illuminate. I always thought hindsight gave history teachers the most lopsided advantage over pretty much everybody they ever talked about, but Jake was rather modest in his infallibility just the same.

In more practical terms the wrong side of our history was in the southwest corner of the room, where the window was drafty and the overhead light flickered like in a disco. I sat behind June and rubbed her shoulders when the wind blew, and that buzzing overhead fluorescent was a kind of sound track to our little wrong-side romance. Bzzzz.

The point, though, was that the back of English, the wrong side of history, wherever we were in May was a better place than where we were just a few weeks later, and I am none the wiser still as to why.

Bad overhead lighting makes me melancholy now.

PETE
HAUTMAN

Transcending stories of life-changing friendship from Benjamin Alire Sáenz

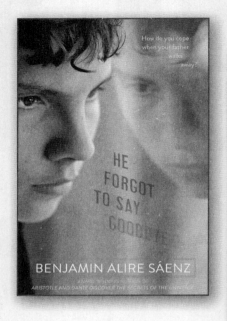

The inspirational memoir of a teenager who saved a Congresswoman's life

"I met Daniel Hernandez and came away feeling invigorated about America's future. We all watched Daniel in an incredible moment of heroism. Now, he's made a life of service and whether he stays in local politics or hits the national stage, he will inspire America for a long time."

—ERIN BURNETT, CNN news anchor

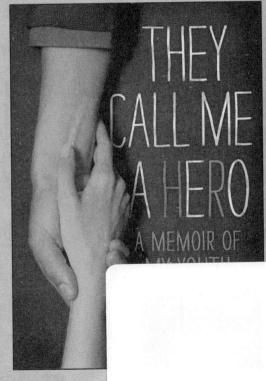

EBOOK AND SPANISH LANGUAGE EDITION

SIMON & SCHUSTER BFYR

TEEN.SimonandSchuster.com